You Said You Loved Me
By Kelli N. Bolton

You Said You Loved Me
Copyright © 2009 Kelli Bolton
All rights reserved

All Scripture references that do not have the Bible version noted are the author's paraphrase.

ISBN: **978-0-615-37187-0**

Published by:
Bolton Press, LLC/Kelli Bolton
P.O. BOX 297892 Columbus, Ohio 43229
kbolton@kelliwrites.com

Cover Design by:
Jeffrey Roberts/Lobo Awards & Graphix

FALL AGAIN

Healing
By Kelly Price

This book is dedicated
to the young people, those that I know personally and
those that I have not yet met. I wanted to give you
something that would cause you to know what "real
love" is. God created you for greatness, not to be abused
and misused.
My prayer is that this book will speak to you in such a
way, that you will know without a doubt there is a God
and He does care about you and what you are going
through.

Acknowledgements

I thank God for finding me to be a worthy vessel to reach the youth of this generation. I am humbly honored and blessed to be a part of the awesome plan that You have for them.

I thank my husband for his love, support and encouragement. Your help and understanding means the world to me. I love you very much.
Also, to my children, for giving me feedback into the lives of the youth today.

To the youth of A.F.W.C, thank you for supporting your youth leader, and offering words of encouragement.

To my family and friends that have spoken words of love, support and blessings over me and my book. There are not enough words to say thank you.

For my prayer partners who have gone to the enemy's camp and took back everything that he has stolen from me concerning this project. I thank you more than these words can express.

To Jessica, Mina and Shawmeen, thanks for your help and being my extra set of eyes and hands through this process.

To Pastor Tolliver and the members of Agape Family Worship Center, I love you all and thank you for your support.

CHAPTER ONE

It's the beginning of fall semester at Virtue Christian Academy, one of the premier Christian schools in Rhema, Ohio. As students walk the freshly painted hallways, there is an exciting buzz in the air. Some were laughing while others were shaking their heads in disbelief. The drama that had taken place yesterday afternoon was not typically experienced at Virtue Academy. As the number one Christian school in Ohio, it was known for its diverse student population, outstanding academic success and student conduct that exceeded expectations of staff, parents and the school board, until yesterday.

"Is it true?" Brianna asked.

"That's what I heard," Casey responded.

"How long have they been dating and where did she meet this guy, thugzrus.com?" Brianna asked as she walked to her locker.

"That's beside the point. He had no right to do that to her," Casey replied shoving her books into her book bag.

"I didn't say it was okay..." Brianna began in defense of her question.

"Shush, here comes Kayla now."

All eyes turn to watch Kayla as she walks down the hallway. Tall and slender, she holds her head high in confidence, her navy and gold uniform crisp and clean.

"Good morning ladies," she says with a grin as she stops at Brianna's locker.

Staring at Kayla in disbelief, Casey and Brianna ask at the same time, "Are you okay?"

With a self-assured grin she replies, "Of course I'm okay, it was nothing. We fight all the time."

"All of the time?" Casey asked.

"Yes, it just got a little out of hand this time because I said I wanted to go out with someone else who would treat me better. He got really mad, spit in my face and shoved me into a locker. I got up and threw my can of pop at the back of his head." She begins to laugh. "His head was so hard that it caused the can to explode."

"I'm just concerned about you Kayla," Brianna observed. "If you can tell him that you're going to find someone else, then there is obviously a problem within this relationship. Besides, you are only in the ninth grade. You don't need to be getting so serious anyway."

"There you go with that self-righteous attitude. You take Bible class way too serious."

With concern in her voice Casey stops Kayla. "Maybe you should take it seriously. It can only help you."

Rolling her eyes as she walks off, Kayla replies over her shoulder, "Whatever."

As she turns the corner and walks up the stairs, Kayla sees something she never expected. Mark, the guy she just broke up with the day before, was laughing with another girl in the hallway.

Her heart begins to race and a knot forms in her throat. "Mark?" she calls.

"What," he responds coldly. The other girl looks over at Kayla and walks away. "What's going on here, who is she?" demanded Kayla as she watches the other girl go down the hall.

Mark turns toward her with anger in his eyes. "You got a lot of nerve asking me who that is; especially when you said you were going to find someone else. If you can do it so can I. I'm done with you." He turns to walk away.

"Wait, you're done with me?" Kayla asks following Mark down the hall not fully understanding what just happened.

"You heard me, now get somewhere and leave me alone."

"You said you loved me," Kayla fumed trying to catch her breath through tears.

"Yeah I said it," Mark replied with a sly smirk across his face, "but I guess I didn't really mean it."

As he shrugs his shoulders and turns to walk away, Kayla suddenly takes off running full speed, jumping onto Mark's back, biting, scratching and punching him.

He swings her around, grabbing at her hands trying to

stop her attack. Kayla grabs Mark around the neck

determined not to let go.

At the same time Mr. Chase, the school principal, was

making his rounds through the hallways. "Mr.

Brown," he yells into his radio. "Please come to the

second floor, south side I need assistance!"

Within seconds the school resource officer comes to the

aid of Mr. Chase. As Mr. Brown holds onto Kayla, she

lunges at Mark.

"I HATE YOU!" she screams.

"Young lady, get a hold of yourself and go to my

office," Mr. Chase said firmly.

"You better be glad I don't hit girls," Mark snaps as he wipes blood from his face. Kayla scratched him up pretty good.

"Go to my office now and don't say another word," Mr. Chase shouted.

His tone moved both students into action. Kayla wipes her face, straightens up her clothes and walks downstairs to the principal's office. Mrs. Rivers, the school secretary, is busy tending to a new student when Kayla walks through the door.

"What do you need Kayla?" she asks.

"Mr. Chase sent me in here," Kayla replied.

"Well have a seat until he gets here."

Kayla sits down in the chair right next to the office door. The sound of the fax machine receiving incoming faxes seemed louder than usual to Kayla this day. The phone was ringing non-stop and the mail carrier had just delivered the morning mail. Fuming, she thinks about things Mark had told her over the past three months.

"Were they all a bunch of lies?" she thought out loud.

"Why would he do that?"

"Kayla Michaels?"

"Yes?" She turns her head as a woman approaches her slowly.

"My name is Ms. Sanders and I'm the ninth grade guidance counselor. Mr. Chase asked me to come to talk with you."

Guarded Kayla responds, "Talk about what?"

"To find out what caused the confrontation between you and another student."

Kayla reluctantly gets up and follows after Ms. Sanders. She shuffles her feet as they walk around the corner to the guidance office. Ms. Sanders opens the door and offers Kayla a seat.

Meanwhile, Mr. Chase is talking with Mark outside the nurse's office.

"Young man, you know the rules here at Virtue Christian Academy. You don't fight and most importantly, you never hit a young lady. Have you lost your mind?" Mr. Chase scolds Mark as they walk back to his office. Mark drops his hand away from the band aid the nurse has placed on his neck and sighs.

"I didn't do anything Mr. Chase, she jumped on me. She's the one that lost her mind."

"What happened?" Mr. Chase asked; concerned about what would cause Kayla to attack Mark.

"Look, I was flexing my muscles a little bit while talking to another girl in the hallway. As we're standing there laughing Kayla comes up to me with an attitude. I told

her that we were through and turned to walk away.

She went crazy and started hitting and scratching me."

"Did you tell her you two were no longer dating?" Mr.

Chase asked him.

"She knew after yesterday when she hit me in the head

with a can of pop. And it still hurts," Mark replied

while rubbing the spot where the can hit him.

"I'm going to have to sit down with both of your

parents and discuss this issue. We teach our students

here at Virtue Christian Academy to walk in character

and integrity, to be accountable and respectful to one

another and all authority figures. I did not see that this

morning, and I want to get to the bottom of this. Do

you understand?"

"Yes"

As they enter into the main office, Mr. Chase asks Mrs. Rivers for a hall pass.

"Take this and go straight to class young man."

"Yes Mr. Chase," Mark replies as he takes the pass and heads out the door.

Back in the guidance counselor's office, Ms. Sanders is questioning Kayla. "You are a new student this year correct?" she asks while flipping through Kayla's file.

"Yes."

"You were granted a scholarship to attend Virtue Academy…."

"What does that have to do with anything?" Kayla snapped.

"Well, as a scholarship student you signed a student conduct form as all students did and it states that any acts of violence could be grounds for expulsion"

"You mean I could get kicked out?" Kayla asked with

much anxiety in her voice. She paces back and forth

before Ms. Sanders nervously ringing her hands.

Nodding her head, Ms. Sanders replied, "Yes Kayla."

"What can I do to make this right? My mom will kill

me if I get kicked out."

Ms. Sanders encourages Kayla to take a seat and pulls a

brochure from her desk drawer.

"Well, there is a group that you can attend for domestic

violence."

"Domestic violence," Kayla interrupts. "There is no

domestic violence in my relationship with Mark. That's

crazy."

Ms. Sanders stands up, walks over to Kayla and sits

down beside her.

"Kayla, anytime you have to put your hands on another person to get them to pay attention to you or get your way, that isn't good. Resorting to violence is not the way to handle a disagreement."

Slouching down in the chair with her head tilted back, Kayla let's out a long sigh.

"So what am I supposed to do now?" she asked.

"Well, you could start by first apologizing for your behavior to Mr. Chase and Mark," Ms. Sanders suggested.

"You want me to apologize to him?" Kayla asked while rolling her eyes. "Yeah right; I ain't got that to do."

"If you don't, this will only make the situation worse."

"What else can I do?" she asks disregarding this suggestion.

"Acknowledge you have some issues and that you may need some help" Ms. Sanders told her.

"There's nothing wrong with defending yourself Ms. Sanders."

"Did he put his hands on you first?"

"No."

"So why did you put your hands on him?"

"He disrespected me by talking to some other girl."

"Oh I see. You needed to show him that he couldn't get away with treating you that way."

"Now you hear me," Kayla replies as she throws a few punches in the air to show that she's tough.

"But Kayla, that's called *control*. You were trying to control the situation between the two of you and resorted to violence when that didn't work. So you see you *do* need help dealing with your emotions."

"I guess I never thought of it that way," she replied, slumping back down in the chair turning to stare out the window.

"What are you thinking about Kayla?"

As she looks at Ms. Sanders tears roll down her cheeks.

"How could he say that he loves me and we end up here?"

"Kayla, I don't have the answer to that, but I do have another view of what love is to share with you."

She hands Kayla a Bible. "Turn to I Corinthians chapter 13 and start at verse 4, ending at verse 8."

As she reads over the verses, Kayla weeps uncontrollably allowing the Bible to fall to the floor. Ms. Sanders puts her arm around Kayla and holds her as she tries to speak.

"I guess he never really loved me according to what the Bible describes."

"Did you love him according to what the Bible said?"

"I thought I did but if it says love never fails then I guess we didn't have 'real love'."

Wiping her face with the tissue Ms. Sanders had given her, she starts to say something else when a knock at the door interrupts her.

"Come in," Ms. Sanders answered.

Mr. Chase walks into the office followed by a tall dark skinned woman. It's Mrs. Valerie Michaels, Kayla's mother, and she is not happy. She had to leave work to come to the school and was embarrassed having to explain this to her boss.

"Mom, I can explain..." Kayla begins but quickly shuts her mouth as her mother shoots her a disapproving look.

"There is no excuse for this type of behavior. Do you know you could lose your scholarship?" she interrupts. The muscles in her face were visibly tense as she glared intensely at her only child.

"Let's sit down and discuss this situation," Mr. Chase intervenes while pulling up a chair for Mrs. Michaels. Smiling faintly as she thanks Mr. Chase for the chair, she sits down without taking her eyes off of Kayla.

"I was wrong," Kayla blurts out trying to plead her case. "I was angry with Mark for him telling me that our relationship was over."

"What relationship? You told me the two of you were just friends."

"It started out that way, and then about a month ago he asked me to be his girlfriend."

"I didn't send you to a Christian school to become violent. I sent you here because I thought you needed a more positive environment, something better than the school you've attended for the last three years. And now this happens..." Mrs. Michael's voice trails off as she angrily turns to face Mr. Chase. "What's going on around here? Do you allow your students to just act out any time they feel like it?"

"Now Mrs. Michaels, I will have to stop you right there," Mr. Chase began, causing her to lighten her tone. "Both you and Kayla attended the freshman orientation and signed the student code of conduct. As her parent it is your responsibility to teach what acceptable behavior to display in school. It is our job to reinforce what has already been taught."

"Are you saying I haven't taught my child how to act in public?" She asked getting defensive.

"No Mrs. Michaels," Mr. Chase replies in a less defensive tone. "What I am saying is that you cannot expect a school to do everything when it comes to behaviors that should be taught in the home."

"Kayla knows right from wrong. This, this boy has gotten her off track."

"I have to take responsibility for my actions," Kayla interrupts. "This whole situation is just messed up and I'm sorry. Please don't kick me out of school, I really like it here."

"May I make a suggestion?" Ms. Sanders chimes in.

"Instead of possible expulsion, I think Kayla might benefit from attending an anger management relationship session offered at the community center. They also provide a session which talks about domestic violence within a relationship. Once she receives some counseling on this issue, we can meet again to discuss her progress or to decide if further punishment is needed."

"Why does she need to attend this type of class after a simple spat between two kids?" Mrs. Michaels asked, concerned that this would hurt Kayla's chances of attending another school in the future.

"It was more than a spat Mrs. Michaels. Kayla jumped on this young man's back and attacked him like a wild animal. And yesterday, she hit him in the head with a can of pop," Mr. Chase explained while looking over at Kayla.

"He pushed me into a locker and I fell. So when I got up that was all I could do as he walked away. He deserved it." Kayla blurted out, trying to defend herself.

"He didn't tell me that part and I will address that with him."

"Are you going to make him attend this class as well?" Mrs. Michaels questioned.

"Both of them will be required to attend classes, but let's focus on Kayla right now. I made the suggestion because I think it is important for Kayla and other young girls to know what a healthy relationship looks like. Whether a person is saved or not they should know that being in a relationship doesn't give them or anyone else the right to be hit, kicked or pushed," explained Ms. Sanders. "I had Kayla read I Corinthians 13:4-8 to show her what God says about love and she confessed she really didn't know what love meant. Our young people get misinformation all of the time, whether it be from peers, TV, music or most importantly the adults in their lives. It's time we showed them what love really is and what it is not."

Mrs. Michaels looks at Kayla and asks her, "What do you think?"

"I guess it can't hurt to learn about something that's going to help me."

"Mr. Chase, I will speak with my pastor to see if he can talk with Kayla as well. Thank you for your help," she says as she stands and shakes his hand.

"Ms. Sanders, thank you for being such a positive influence here."

"You're welcome Mrs. Michaels."

As they walk into the hallway, Mrs. Michaels addresses Kayla. "When you go back to class young lady, you'd better not say one word to anyone about this. I will deal with you when I get home."

"Yes ma'am. Can we still go shopping afterwards?"

With an evil glare, Mrs. Michaels answers coldly, "You better pray that you will remember what it's like to shop after I'm through with you."

Kayla drops her head and walks toward the stairs knowing that she has made a big mistake.

"I don't understand teenagers these days. It's like they don't think before they speak," Mrs. Michaels says in response to Kayla's nonchalant attitude. Turning toward Mr. Chase and Ms. Sanders as they stand in the doorway, Mrs. Michaels cheerfully says, "Have a nice afternoon Mr. Chase and Ms. Sanders."

"Enjoy the rest of your morning Mrs. Michaels."

Rushing out to her car, Mrs. Michaels looks at her watch seeing that she has a half-hour to get back to work. Muttering to herself about Kayla's selfish behavior, she peels out of the parking lot heading back to her office. Brianna and Casey run up to Kayla before their next class.

"Girl are you crazy?" Brianna starts in. "Why in the world are you hittin a dude as big as Mark?"

"I'm not allowed to talk about it right now, text me later and I'll tell you what happened. I'm in a lot of trouble and only prayer can get me out."

"Well it's a good thing we're going to Bible class. You'll have all the time to pray then," Casey replies with a giggle. As the girls walk toward the classroom, they pass by a couple of Mark's friends standing at his locker. Chaz, light – complexion, tall and slender with a gold chain around his neck and braids, rolls his eyes at Kayla as she walks by. Ricardo, Puerto Rican, short and stocky, picks out his afro while waiting for Mark to come down the hallway. He was the newest addition to their ninth grade class.

"Hey man, I heard your girl went psycho on you," Chaz remarks as he leans against the wall with a smile. "You got beat by a girl."

"Man please, she did not beat me. I threw her off of me. Besides, I'm done with her," Mark replies, walking by them both as if they were invisible.

"So I guess she didn't take it too well," Ricardo

inquired, more concerned with his friend's actions than

was Chaz.

"She'll get over it. You know my swag, you know how

I do, love 'em and leave 'em."

"Man you ain't right."

Mark smiles, "Pray for me and maybe I'll get right."

"Be careful what you ask for, you just might get it.

Come on before we're late for Bible class." Ricardo

waits impatiently for his friend as Mark grabs his book

bag. Slamming his locker shut he and his friends sprint

down the hall to Bible class. The tardy bell rings just as

they take their seats. Catching his breath, Mark notices

Kayla looking over in his direction. Ignoring her gaze

he rubs the back of his head and turns to focus on Ms.

Grace. Wearing a long navy blue dress with a gold scarf

around her neck, Ms. Grace walks in front of the class and begins her lecture.

Kayla glances over at Mark and sees that he's purposely turned his back to her. She wonders if she made the right choice in telling him that she loved him. She thought she did but now she had some doubts. Their relationship only lasted for three months but she believed he was the one for her. Now all she could think about was what happened earlier and feelings of guilt and shame began to settle in. Kayla faces forward in her seat trying hard to concentrate on today's lesson.

"If you could take out your Bibles and turn to Matthew chapter 12, verse 36, we are going to discuss accountability today. Does anyone know what it is to be accountable?" Ms. Grace asks the class.

"Being responsible for your actions," Casey replied.

"You are right. Let's read together please."

"But I tell you that men will have to give account on the Day of Judgment for every careless word they have spoken."

"Would anyone care to summarize this passage of scripture?"

"I think it means you will be judged for the things you say," Kayla answered.

"You are correct Kayla. Everyone will have to give an account for their words that did not produce good fruit, or positive actions."

"You mean like someone saying that they love you and then you find out it's a lie?" Kayla asked.

The class begins to snicker and giggle. Chaz and Ricardo look over at Mark.

"Well, that could be used as an example. But if God is love, He doesn't want His people hurting and lying to one another." Ms. Grace looks slowly over at Kayla as she tries to move forward with the lesson.

"Then can someone tell me why people lie to those they are supposed to love?"

"Kayla, this seems to have struck a nerve with you. We can address that a little later. Right now I must finish this lesson before the bell rings."

Kayla agrees with a nod of her head. The classroom falls silent with only the occasional rustling of pages as students rush to complete their assignment. Ms. Grace stands to her feet as the bell rings, signaling the start of the lunch period.

"Please remember to read the rest of Matthew 12," she announces as the students turn in their paperwork.

"We will discuss it tomorrow. Also, for today's lunch you will have a choice of cheese, sausage or pepperoni pizza. The first slice is free but you'll have to pay extra for additional slices."

Chaz and Ricardo give one another a high five as they exit the classroom.

"Brianna, are you eating your regular chicken and fries, or will you try the pizza?" Casey asks as she puts her Bible and notebook in her book bag.

"I'm not sure. I might try something new. What about you Kayla?"

"I'm going to stay after to talk with Ms. Grace. I'll catch up with you later."

"Okay."

Brianna and Casey head to the lunchroom as Kayla approaches Ms. Grace.

"Ms. Kayla, what's going on with you?" Ms. Grace asks while erasing the blackboard. "You know my classroom cannot be used as a talk show forum for you to air your personal business." Putting the eraser down she turns to find Kayla staring silently at the floor.

"I'm sorry Ms. Grace. Mark and I just broke up and I'm bothered by his attitude. He told me he loved me but now acts as if I mean nothing to him."

"Do you know him well enough to say that you loved him?" Ms. Grace motions for Kayla to sit in the chair beside her desk.

"I guess not. He said it to me and I felt like I really did love him."

"Tell me Kayla, how did this relationship develop and how did it end?"

"Well, we met at freshmen orientation in July. He was tall, dark and handsome and his locker was right next to mine. We started talking and since school hadn't started yet, we just exchanged phone numbers. A couple of weeks after school began he wanted me to become his girlfriend. Mark was the first guy to ask me out so I thought he really liked me."

"Did you two have sex?"

"No!" Kayla shouted. "I do have some morals."

Ms. Grace laughs for a moment and then turning serious asks, "Okay, so if you never had sex with him why are you angry? You haven't lost anything but time."

"I'm angry because he told me he loved me, and then later said he never meant it." Kayla snapped, folding her arms in frustration.

"Kayla, love is not supposed to make you angry. You need to read your Bible and find out what God says about love and how important you are to Him."

"I already know. Ms. Sanders had me read I Corinthians 13 and that definition of love was quite different from what I thought. I guess I just liked him a lot."

As the bell begins to ring, Kayla realizes that she has missed lunch.

"I really don't mind," she thought to herself. "There are other things I need to deal with and food isn't one of them."

As she continues throughout her day, Kayla's mind wonders about the true meaning of love. Before her father left, he used to tell her every night that he loved her. But now he wasn't there and she really missed that.

"My parents aren't together anymore. Mark and I are no longer together….." Kayla takes a deep breath and sighs. They used to talk on the phone everyday and he would always text, "I LUV U", to her at night. She wondered how these relationships could change so quickly over night.

As the school day draws to a close, Kayla puts her things in her locker and heads outside to catch her bus. Waving bye to her friends, she's greeted with the 'wonderful' smell of motor oil and vanilla air freshener as she makes her way back to her assigned seat in the fifth row. As the bus travels through her old neighborhood, Kayla looks longingly out the window at the house where she used to live happily with her parents. She missed the days of walking the neighborhood with her friends or watching her dad work on his car. Her mother worked long hours, but was always home in time to sit down for dinner and enjoy family time. Shifting her long legs, she looks up with dread as she sees her bus stop approaching. Taking a deep breath, Kayla puts on her book bag and slowly heads up the aisle to exit the bus. Kayla walked home with her friends in her old neighborhood, so riding the bus was new for her, but she didn't seem to mind. It allowed her to leave the old neighborhood and all the good memories behind a little quicker. Feeling sad at first, those thoughts left her as she climbed the stairs to her front porch.

CHAPTER TWO

"Mom, I'm home."

"Kayla Marie Michaels, sit down on the couch now!"

her mom said in a voice Kayla was all too familiar with.

Thinking to herself, "She just called me by my

governmentals, this can not be good."

Kayla nervously puts her book bag down and looks

around for her mom, not knowing what to expect.

Coming out of the kitchen wiping her hands with a

towel, Mrs. Michaels begins to speak.

"I've thought long and hard after leaving your school

today about what to do with you."

Kayla's stomach starts turning and flipping as she

begins to remember the last time her mother disciplined

her. It was just two months ago for using profanity at a family cook out.

"Mom…"

"I don't want to hear any excuses. You are going to learn one way or another that your behavior needs to change."

As she comes toward Kayla, Kayla ducks her head and covers her face with her hands. Her mom begins to hit her, first slapping her then hitting her with closed fists.

"Mom, Mom, stop. You're hurting me."

"You should have thought about that earlier," she sneered as she swung her arms wildly hitting Kayla in the back.

Kayla struggles to get up and runs upstairs to her room. She locks the door behind her knowing that her mother would soon be there to beat on her some more.

"This door can't save you," Mrs. Michaels yells while pressing her body up against the door. "You'd better come out or I'm coming in there!"

To her surprise the door suddenly opens and she sees Kayla standing there flat footed, glaring back at her mother.

"Do you think you can whip me?" Mrs. Michaels asks while clenching her fist. She'd challenged her daughter many times in the past and had never lost a fight.

Kayla doesn't answer but continues to stare at her mother. Spots of blood dot the gold blouse of her uniform.

"I hope you don't think you are going to hit me like you did that boy-you must not know..." Mrs. Michaels begins.

"I used to wonder how I could become so angry that I would hit people," Kayla quietly whispered through clenched teeth, tears running down her face. "Now I know why, my mother hits me when she doesn't like something."

"I am the parent and you will listen to me." Mrs. Michaels takes a step toward Kayla.

Unafraid Kayla steps toward her mother, fist clenched prepared to fight. Seeing her daughter undaunted Mrs. Michaels turns and walks away, looking over her shoulder to see if Kayla was coming after her.

"I'm not through with you young lady. We will talk later but right now I want you to get ready for prayer and Bible study."

Kayla returns to her room and changes out of her uniform. Looking in the mirror to brush her hair, she looks at a picture of her dad atop the dresser. How could she be so mean and act like I did something so wrong Kayla thought? Not sure of what caused her family to separate; she wondered if her mother's behavior was the reason. She never saw her parents argue and her father was always respectful and affectionate toward her and her mother. Slamming the photo face down, Kayla grabs her Bible from out of her book bag and heads downstairs.

On their way to church, Kayla thinks about her day and looks over her recent behavior to examine whether or not she may really have an anger problem. She feels her face tightening up as she remembers her mother standing at her bedroom door threatening her.

"Kayla, Kayla."

She ignores her mother turning to look out the window.

They haven't been to church in six months and she

wondered why they were going now. After her dad left

them, her mom took on longer hours at her job. They

moved into a new neighborhood and had little time left

over for anything else.

"Kayla," Mrs. Michaels begins interrupting her

thoughts. "I don't understand what's going on with

you. Your attitude has changed so much in the past few

months. Are you having problems at school? Is it peer

pressure? Tell me...let me know how to help you,"

Mrs. Michaels pleads as she tries to reach out to her

daughter.

"How can you expect me to talk to you when you beat

me like I stole something from you?" Kayla mumbles.

As they pull into the church parking lot, Mrs. Michaels parks the car. Turning to her daughter she says, "I'm sorry I hurt you but you..."

"You say you're sorry every time you do it," Kayla interrupts her with tears welling up in her eyes. "Now we end up here at church like everything is supposed to be okay. I'm tired of pretending. I'm going to talk to Pastor Lee whether you like it or not."

She unlocks her car door and races towards the church. It was an older building with colorful stained glass windows and small steps leading to the front door. As she opened the doors and stepped inside, Kayla smiled and relaxed. She enjoyed the sense of peace and love she felt every time she came into the building. They were a small congregation and everyone knew one another. Their youth department was always hosting fun and exciting activities. The young people were really energetic and enthusiastic about sharing their faith with their friends, family and who ever would listen.

"Hey Miss Kayla, how are you?" Sister Lissy, one of the church greeters asks as she comes through the doors.

"I'm okay." Looking past Sister Lissy she asks, "Is Pastor Lee here?"

"Yes he's in his office. Do you want me to get him for you?"

"No thanks. I need to speak with him," she replies and hurries down the hallway. The choir is rehearsing in the sanctuary and Kayla pauses for a moment to listen.

"Knock, knock."

As Pastor Lee looks up from his Bible, his eyes brighten as he receives her with a warm smile. "Come in Kayla," he booms with a great baritone voice.

She slowly enters his office, still marveling at how a man so dark in complexion could have such pearly white teeth.

"It is good to see you. How have you been?"

"Not good," Kayla replied while taking a seat. "I don't know how I got here…" she begins to cry.

Walking over with a box of tissues, Pastor Lee takes a seat beside Kayla concerned.

"What's going on Kayla?" he asks her.

Trying to regain her composure, she wipes her face and begins to share with him all that had happened earlier that day.

"Excuse me Pastor Lee," Mrs. Michaels interjects while standing in the doorway. "I believe I need to be a part of this meeting." She glances nervously over at her daughter as she enters the room.

"Hello Sister Valerie. Kayla was just telling me what happened in school today."

Kayla stares at her mother and says, "My mother beats me."

Staring back at her daughter without blinking Mrs. Michaels responds, "I discipline her for her disobedience and defiant behavior."

Pastor Lee looks at Kayla and then at Valerie in surprise. "Valerie, why don't you take a seat over there," Pastor Lee points toward a chair across from Kayla. "I'm going to speak to both of you about this but first I need to find my wife. I want her to be a part of this discussion.

"Sister Banks," Pastor Lee phones the church secretary, "could you find Sister Lee and tell her she is needed in my office." Hanging up the phone he turns to Kayla. "Go on to the restroom and clean your face. Spend some time in the youth department's classroom until I'm through talking to your mother."

Turning toward Mrs. Michaels, Pastor Lee asks, "Sister Valerie will you wait in the sanctuary until my wife can join us?"

Just then Sister Velva Lee walks in. "Good evening Sister Valerie how are you?" she asks as she gives Kayla a big hug. The light scent of perfume fills the room as she greets her husband with a small pat on the shoulders. Sensing something is wrong; she closes the office door and takes a seat next to her husband. Sister

Lee was not only the pastor's wife but she also lead the

women's ministry.

Kayla sat quietly in front of her mother as Mrs. Michaels

nervously replied, "I've been better. My daughter and I

are going through a difficult time right now and we

need some guidance."

"Well I pray that you will find what you need here,"

Sister Lee replied as she reached out to grasp her hand.

"Okay honey, let's pray." She motions for her husband

to begin after they all hold hands.

Pastor Lee prays for insight, wisdom and direction

while conducting this meeting.

"Valerie," Pastor Lee begins after the prayer is over,

"tell me why Kayla would say that you beat her?"

"We were all raised getting our butts whipped when we got out of line, so that's what I do with her. She thinks she's too old to get a whipping," she replies with a nonchalant attitude. Valerie was raised in a time where the children were not only disciplined by their parents, but by other adults in the community as well. So after the neighbor punished you, they told your parents and you got whipped again after they left. Getting a spanking was nothing new, so she couldn't understand why she was being questioned on how she disciplined Kayla.

"I agree there needs to be discipline in a household but it doesn't need to get out of control where it turns into abuse. Do you agree?"

"Yes," Mrs. Michaels replies.

"So how often does Kayla get disciplined?"

Mrs. Michaels doesn't answer. For the first time she fears what others will say about how she punishes Kayla. Her actions could be misunderstood and child protective services might be called.

"Is there something wrong Sister Valerie?" Pastor Lee inquires.

"She gets disciplined as I see fit. It's not an everyday thing," she snaps.

"Would you say it happens on a weekly basis?"

"It just depends," Mrs. Michaels replies, avoiding the question.

"Sister Valerie I have to ask you, do you really have a justifiable reason to punish your daughter...as often as you see fit?"

Becoming defensive she responds, "What I do in my house is my business. I don't ask you how you discipline your children."

"No, you don't, but my children are not here accusing me of abuse."

Silence fills the room.

"Kayla, let's go get something to drink from out of the kitchen." Sister Lee moves her toward the door and into the hallway.

After getting some water, Sister Lee leaves Kayla in the youth department's classroom next door and returns down the hall to the pastor's office. Kayla finds Pastor Charles in the back office sitting at his desk reviewing Sunday's service. He is in charge of the youth and young adults ministry. His office was warmly decorated in navy and gold, the colors of his alma mater, Virtue Christian Academy.

"Well hello Miss Kayla, how are you?" Pastor Charles asks pleasantly surprised to see Kayla back at church.

"Very confused Pastor Charles," Kayla replies taking a seat in one of his plush blue lounge chairs, restraining herself from reclining in it.

"Do you want to talk?"

"I've been talking all day and I don't seem to be getting anywhere but into more trouble."

"Well if you don't want to talk, can you help me put these packets in order for tonight's lesson?" he asks while handing Kayla a stack of papers.

She begins separating the stacks and with her back turned she begins, "I don't know what I'm doing anymore."

"What do you mean?" Pastor Charles asks as he files each stack into separate folders.

"I can't seem to make anyone happy. Not my mom, not Mark. Is God even happy with me at this point?"

Pastor Charles puts down the folders and softly puts his hand on Kayla's shoulder. "Do you want to talk now?"

Nodding her head yes, she and Pastor Charles sit down. Even though he was in his thirties Kayla had always felt at ease when in his presence. He counseled many of the young people, not only in the church but at Virtue Christian Academy as well. And it didn't hurt that all of the girls thought he was cute.

"Tell me why you think your mom and God are unhappy with you. And who is Mark?"

"Mark was my boyfriend until yesterday. He told me that he loved me but now he acts like I don't even exist." Rolling her eyes she continues, "My relationship with my mom is horrible. I get in trouble if I even breathe wrong at home. And I honestly can't tell you the last time I prayed before today."

"Well would you like to pray now?"

"It's been so long I don't think God would even recognize my voice."

Chuckling, Pastor Charles replies, "He hasn't forgotten you Kayla. I'll pray…"

They pray and Kayla starts to cry.

"I used to be able to pray and God would answer me. Now it's like His line is busy."

"Kayla what's going on at home? It has been awhile since you last attended one of our youth services. Are you busy involved in sports or other things with your school?"

Wiping her face she replies, "No. Since my mom and dad split she works two jobs now. We've moved to a new neighborhood and I don't know anyone I could ask that would be able to bring me to service on Wednesdays." Kayla hesitates before continuing, "Mom is trippin and has started beating me. I know I mess up sometimes but not that bad."

"When you say she beats you, is this often?" Pastor Charles asks with concern in his eyes.

"I don't know Pastor Charles. I would say more than normal, at least once or twice every other week. Nothing makes her happy anymore and I have to make it up to her by letting her beat me like a runaway slave."

Sitting back in his chair he asks, "What are some of the things you're getting punished for?"

"Leaving dishes in the sink is one thing. She makes them dirty after I've washed them and I feel if I have to clean up after myself, why can't she? If I have my headphones on while listening to music, she accuses me of tuning her out. Or if someone calls and I ask who it is, she thinks I'm trying to be nosey." Kayla pauses to catch her breath, "I got into a little fight with my boyfriend at school and she was called in for a conference. She acted like she was concerned in front of the principal and guidance counselor but she went crazy and started beaten' me with her fists after I got home. All I could do was run to my room. I was so mad at this point, knowing that she would come after me, that I confronted her. I was ready to fight her if I had to. She knew it and walked away to calm down. Then she tells me to get ready for church like nothing happened. Once we got here I told her I was going to tell Pastor Lee what was going on and I ran to his office. She comes in and acts like I'm so wrong, so I started sharing what was going on. Pastor Lee told me to come down here while he and Sister Lee meet with my mom. So now you know what's been goin on with me."

"Sounds like you've had a lot happening Miss Kayla. I'll let Pastor Lee intervene between you and your mom...but tell me more about this boyfriend of yours. You said his name was Mark?" Pastor Charles asks with a sly smile.

"Pastor Charles," she smiles shyly.

"What, you can't talk to me about boys?" he asks.

"Well tell me this, does he attend church here?"

"No, we met at school. He was so cute and I was just dumb. Now I'm hurt because he told me that he loved me but he didn't mean it. So when I saw him talking to another girl, I went off on him and I let him know that he can't play me and get away with it." Kayla sits back in the chair with a smirk and cracks her knuckles.

"So now you go around starting fights just to show you're hard?" Pastor Charles asked in a disapproving tone.

"No Pastor Charles. Yesterday, he spit in my face and pushed me against some lockers, so I retaliated by throwing a can of pop at his head. When I saw him talking to that girl this morning, he tried to act like he didn't know me and that made me mad. I went off on him and now they want me to go to some anger management, domestic violence class offered at the community center."

"That sounds like a positive step in the right direction."

"I guess."

"Will your mother be attending these classes with you?"

Pastor Charles asked cautiously. "From what you've

shared with me I have some concerns for your safety as

well as your mother's."

"Perhaps she should," Kayla replied as she finished

putting the papers together.

As a group of young people began filing into the room

for Bible class, Kayla quietly takes a seat in the back,

listening attentively as Pastor Charles begins to teach.

"Hey Kayla," Mya whispers as she leans over in her

chair. "We haven't seen you around here in a long

time." As she gives Kayla a hug, Kayla replies, "My

mom is working a lot so I don't get out much."

"Take my phone number," she pauses to write it down

on a piece of paper, "and I can come get you since I'm

driving now." Mya and Kayla have been friends since Kayla joined the church five years ago, so Mya was shocked when Kayla suddenly stopped attending. She was also a little hurt when Kayla no longer returned her phone calls and text messages, so she was very happy to see her friend back in Bible class.

Mya gives Kayla her number and smiles while jiggling her car keys in her hand.

"Okay."

"Let's begin with a recap from last week's lesson…"

Pastor Charles begins as the young people open up their packets.

CHAPTER THREE

"Dude, I heard you and your girl was goin at it today," Antonio shouts while walking across the street toward Mark. Antonio caught up to Mark as they were leaving school.

"Man, you know I don't let no girl act up on me. I handles my business."

"So what's up? Are you two still together?"

"Naw man, I've moved on."

"So what happened?" Antonio asked while they head to the corner store for their after school favorites.

"She started crying saying she wanted to spend more time with me...like we was all serious," Mark replied.

"So I started ignoring her. She tells me she can find someone else. I felt like she was trying me, so I had to show her what happens when you disrespect me. I spit in her face and pushed her into the lockers."

"You did what!" Antonio exclaimed shocked at what was coming out of his friend's mouth. "Mark, the whole school was talking about it."

"When she got up, she threw a can of pop at me and it hit me in the head. After that I was done with her."

"Why just because she defended herself?"

Shrugging his shoulders Mark replied, "I guess I'm not used to girls fighting back. What's it to you anyway, you taking up for her?"

"No, I'm just trying to figure out what's going on with you. From the marks on your face, she did more than throw pop at you."

"This morning she saw me talking to Nina, that cute Latino girl, and she went psycho jumping on me and acting crazy. Mr. Chase and Mr. Brown had to hold me back."

"So you tellin me you would have hit her?" Antonio asks while grabbing a bag of chips and a liter of pop off of the shelf.

"Why not, she hit me. Besides, that's all the guys on TV do to get their girls to act right."

Mark grabs the bag of chips from Antonio and races to the cash register.

"That's just TV man," Antonio replied as he slaps his friend in the back of the head. "Most of it's not real and the ones who do abuse their girlfriends or wives have lots of money to get them off the hook, or they buy their victims a gift."

"Well listen to you like you all Mr. Perfect. You're only two years older than me." Mark glares over at his friend as he rubs his head in agony.

"And with age comes wisdom. Besides, my parents taught me better than that. You go to a Christian school now so you should know better."

"Just because I go to a Christian school doesn't mean me and my girl won't have problems. Everyone wants me to be so perfect and I do try, but I am who I am. No school is going to change that."

"You're right; it truly will have to be an act of God." Laughing, they leave the store and Antonio crosses the street. "I'll see you later man."

"Alright," Mark smiles as he watches his friend turn the corner.

Strolling down the street, ducking the hanging tree limbs, he wonders what he will tell his parents when he gets home. Earlier in the year, his parents had given their lives over fully to the Lord and their new attitude was hard for him to adjust to. They have completely changed starting first with the music that they listened to, and now they've changed the shows that they watch on TV. Mark found the holiness lifestyle boring. He used to like listening to music with his dad as they washed the cars on the weekends. Now all his dad listens to is gospel music and Mark was not a huge fan. He had no problems making this fact known and often did. His family never went to church, and his house was known as the party house among family and friends during the holidays. Now that his parents had given their lives to Christ, they made some changes in their lifestyle and Mark refused to adjust to those changes. He always made an excuse not to attend Bible study and found friends to hang out with on the weekends to avoid going to service on Sundays. His parents didn't want to push the issue but they were getting tired of his increasingly defiant behavior.

Turning the key in the door he hears his mother ask, "Mark, is that you?"

"You know it," he sings back to her.

"Come in here please."

As he walks into the kitchen, Mark sees a man with a tall and familiar muscular frame sitting at his kitchen table opposite his mom. It's Mr. Chase and as he looks from one to the other, he notices a perplexed look on his mother's face.

Looking somewhat surprised he stutters, "What, what are you doin here?"

"You know why I'm here Mark," replied Mr. Chase.

"If it's about that girl, man she's old news." Looking into the refrigerator for something to drink, Mark grabs a can of soda and sits down next to Mr. Chase.

"That may be the case between you two but it's still new to me." Mr. Chase replied.

Looking at her son in exasperation, Mrs. Parks sighs, "Mark, you told me you wouldn't do this again. What's gotten into you?"

"So this isn't the first time he's been in a dispute with a young lady?" Mr. Chase asked in amazement.

"No," replies Mrs. Parks as she stares at her son.

"What happened today and what happened last year are two totally different stories Mom. Why did you even bring that up?"

As Mr. Chase looks at Mark, slightly surprised and disappointed in his lack of respect toward his mother, he asks, "Would you mind sharing with me what happened last year Mrs. Parks?"

Her light brown cheeks darkened slightly as she begins to share what took place. "It was the final day of class at Mark's old school. He and a young lady were joking around until she made a comment on his 'lack of manhood.'"

Mark slurps down the rest of his soda, burping loudly. Mrs. Parks ignores her son and continues, "All of the other students standing around laughed at what she said but Mark took it personally. He walked over to the young lady and slapped her across the face. She fell

against the wall in tears. The principal called his father

and me in to let us know that the girl's parents wanted

to charge Mark with assault. Only after we agreed to

transfer Mark to Virtue Christian Academy did her

parents agree not to pursue the matter."

Mr. Chase sits back in his chair astonished by what he

had just heard.

"You promised me that this wouldn't happen again

Mark. You said you would never hit another girl and

that you would just walk away."

"I did walk away," Mark explained as he walked

around the kitchen. "She attacked me and I just swung

her around to get her off of me."

"So you are here because my son was defending

himself?" Mrs. Parks asked slightly confused.

"No ma'am. Your son hasn't told you about yesterday's confrontation where he spit in the same young lady's face and pushed her against some lockers. This type of behavior has me quite disturbed Mrs. Parks and his actions will not be tolerated as long as he is a student at Virtue Christian Academy."

Pushing away from the table, Mrs. Parks slowly approached her son. "You didn't tell me that you spit in a young lady's face and pushed her into a locker. What is wrong with you? Your father and I raised you better than that!"

Feeling faint, Mrs. Parks begins to fan herself and Mr. Chase hastens to help her sit back down at the kitchen table.

"Man, it was no big deal," Mark sticks his hands in his pocket and leans back against the counter. "She was acting like she could do better than me, so I just had to let her know who I was and that she can't get over on me."

Mr. Chase shakes his head. "Do you hear yourself young man? That is not the way you handle a disagreement."

"That's how my boys in the music videos handle their business. The girls either show them respect or they take it."

"Mark, you know your father and I don't allow you to watch those types of videos. Where do you see these things?"

"I watch videos all the time. Just because you and dad go to church now don't mean I have to change."

The sudden rattle of keys in the front door startles everyone into silence. "Shelly," a man's voice calls, "is someone here?"

"Yes, it's Mark's principal Mr. Chase."

An older and slightly taller version of Mark slowly enters through the kitchen doorway.

"Hello, I'm Michael Parks," he exclaims extending his hand toward Mr. Chase. "I'm Mark's father."

"Gregory Chase sir, nice to meet you," he replies while retuning the handshake.

"What's going on?" he asks looking from his wife to his son.

"I got into a little fight with Kayla at school today."

"It was more than a little fight. I think Mark may need to attend some counseling classes for anger management and domestic violence."

With eyebrows raised in amazement, Mark asks, "Do you think all that is necessary? It was just a little fight."

Mr. Chase explains in a firm tone, "It was not just a little fight Mr. Parks. Your son spit in this young lady's face and pushed her into a locker yesterday. It reached a breaking point this morning. Mark did the right thing by walking away, even after the young lady attacked him. My concern is that Mark shows no remorse in his actions, like it is okay for him to act this way. And from what your wife has shared, this hasn't been the first time he's assaulted someone."

Choosing his words carefully, Mr. Parks responds, "I will address your concerns with my wife and son. I assure you Mr. Chase that he will be dealt with. Thank you for stopping by."

Mr. Parks shows him to the door.

"I will send a referral letter home to be completed for those classes. If Mark does not attend them he will be expelled from Virtue Christian Academy."

As the door closes behind Mr. Chase, Mr. Parks looks over at Mark.

"Go to your room Mark."

"Do I really have to go to those classes dad?"

"You heard what he said. Now go up to your room."

Walking out of the kitchen like nothing ever happened Mark goes to the steps, stops and turns, "I'll go if it will make you happy," he replies with a grin.

"I don't know what to do with him Michael," Mrs. Parks sighs as they watch him go upstairs to his room. "He doesn't listen to me. He said he would never hit another girl after last year's incident and now this. What if Mr. Chase is right? What if Mark has some anger management issues that he needs help to deal with?"

"Well one thing is sure Shelly, he cannot continue with this attitude that it's his right to have control over a person, especially females. Some things are going to have to change." Mr. Parks goes toward the garage to get a box. "Let's start with his music....that mp3 player, his CDs, those will have to go. Next, we will work on removing the cable from off of his TV."

CHAPTER FOUR

"Good morning everyone, my name is Lynn Dean. I am
an advocate here at the Family Life Community Center.
I imagine many of you are not wanting to be here on a
Saturday morning but I promise you will learn some
valuable information if you are open to receive it." As
Lynn ushers the small group into a brightly painted
room, Kayla looks around at the other women. They
take their seats within a semi-circle arrangement
specifically designed to encourage a casual atmosphere
for conversation. Sitting sporadically throughout the
circle, some of the women politely speak while others
remain quiet.

Lynn stands in front of the group and points to a white board behind her which lists the primary rules outlining every group meeting.

"First, let me explain the ground rules we apply prior to each session.

1.) Respect all people whether you agree with them or not.

2.) No judging, put downs or name calling.

3.) No threatening.

4.) Be courteous and listen to the person speaking.

These sound simple enough but we will not be able to accomplish what needs to happen if we don't set some boundaries. Okay now would anyone like to share your name and a little bit about what brought you here today..."

Kayla looks over at her mother as a way to get some reassurance. Valerie stares back at Kayla letting her know that she'd better not say anything to make her look bad. Slowly putting her head down, Kayla begins to wonder if it was even worth being here.

"Well, I'll start and then if you feel like sharing you can. My name is Lynn Dean and I am a survivor of domestic violence. I was married for eight years. Oh it was cool for the first four years until one day my husband lost his job. After being injured he became addicted to pain pills. Then he was getting angry all of the time. I thought at first he was just upset that he couldn't provide for our family and that he would get over it. Well one night he went out with some friends and I didn't think much of it. I was hoping that they could cheer him up because everything I tried seemed to make things worse. He came back home around 2 a.m. and I was in bed asleep. Suddenly I was awakened by a slap to the face. Scared, I jumped up and reached for the gun that we kept in a box under the bed. I heard a voice say, 'You lookin for this?' Squinting through an eye that was beginning to swell shut; I could see him pointing the gun at me. I asked him, 'What's wrong, what did I do?' 'You were born, that's the problem,' was his emotionless reply. He began to hit me with the gun with blows to my head and across my back. I cried, pleading for him to stop. At some point during this attack our daughter Noelle ran into the room, screaming at him to stop. She covered me with her body and he dropped the gun to the floor. This went on over and over again for the last four years of our marriage. Sometimes he wouldn't hit me. He would just yell, call me names or threaten my life. I thought if I could just make him happy then things would get better. They never did and when we would go out with friends, he would act like everything was perfect at home. After talking to a counselor here at the center and trusting in God for strength, I found the courage to walk away from my husband. I took my daughter and everything I could pack in one bag. I've been divorced for three years now and I am slowly making progress to trust people again, to love myself and accept the fact that I am allowed to have peace in my life. My job as an advocate here at Family Life is to help others make positive choices and provide them with the resources that they need. Domestic violence is a serious issue that should never be taken lightly." Pausing briefly for a break to let some of the women compose themselves, Lynn smiles and slowly looks around.

"Now that I have told you about me, who would like to share their story?"

No one speaks at first and Kayla begins to wonder if her mom may have suffered some type of abuse that she never shared before.

She turns to her left as another woman quietly begins to speak, "My life was very similar to yours. My name is Tina Jackson and I recently left my husband of 20 years. He verbally abused me from the day we were married until I finally walked away. I didn't want our children to grow up in that kind of environment so I just left. I stayed for so long because I thought I needed him. Besides," she explained with a roll of the neck with one hand waving in the air, "if he had put his hands on me he knew that would have been the end of him. I have brothers who are in law enforcement. And you think that I would have known better...but he just made me feel like no one else cared and I believed him."

"Thank you for sharing Tina. How many of you have children?" Lynn asked.

Several hands go up in response.

"How many of you think that abuse from your mate affects your children?"

More hands are raised. Valerie and Kayla sit quietly, not participating. Noticing some apprehension Lynn directs her next question to Kayla.

"How old are you?"

"Fifteen."

"Are you aware many young ladies your age are in domestic violence relationships?"

"Yes," she says nodding her head.

"Have you been in one?"

"Yes. I was sent to this class because I attacked my boyfriend after he broke up with me."

All eyes turn to Kayla. Valerie begins to get antsy and interrupts by asking, "What else are we going to do here?" As Lynn looks away from Kayla to address her question, Valerie thinks back on the incident that brought them here. Could her behavior towards her daughter be the reason Kayla has become so angry and aggressive.

Feeling her mother's agitation Kayla begins to shift nervously in her seat.

"Remember the rules," Lynn begins, "respect one another and listen as others share."

"Well she's my daughter and I've heard all this before."

"So why are you here Ms..."

"It's Valerie Michaels and I'm here because our pastor recommended for us to attend one of these sessions."

Smiling, Lynn inquires, "Your pastor must be Pastor Lee."

"Yes."

"He is a great supporter of this cause, something many churches aren't willing to get involved in. I hope that you will take something from this class, whatever the reason that brought you here." Turning her focus back to Kayla, Lynn asks, "What is your name young lady?"

"Kayla."

"Do you know why you were so angry that you attacked this young man?"

"He lied to me and it hurt my feelings. When I saw him in the hallway with another girl I just lost it and went off on him."

"Is that your reaction whenever someone lies to you or rejects you?"

"No, I guess I just acted that way because that's how I've witnessed other people handle their anger." Kayla did not look at her mother as she responded to Lynn's questioning. She did not want to imply that she witnessed this behavior from her.

"Oh, so you've seen other people get upset and hurt people. Did that seem to help the situation or make it worse?"

"It made it worse. And he's been avoiding me every since."

"Well Kayla, I hope to share with you some positive ways in which to deal with your emotions. I thank you for sharing and being honest. Most people would have assumed that you were here because you were a victim, but you have allowed us to see that girls get angry and can be violent too. Would anyone else like to share? We have a few minutes before we leave for our trip."

"What trip?" Kayla speaks up. She looks over at her mother who is just as surprised as she is. Ms. Sanders never mentioned anything about having to take a trip.

"During our first session we will be visiting a place associated with survivors of domestic violence. I can't tell you exactly where we are going, just know it will be an eye opening experience. If there are no other questions, please get your belongings and meet me in the back parking lot to board the van."

"I don't know about this Kayla," Mrs. Michaels says while standing off to the side of the classroom. She wasn't very cooperative during the group session and was uneasy about taking Kayla to a place she knew nothing about. Mrs. Michaels was also a little unnerved by what Kayla had shared during the session. Did the other women in the group think that she was an unfit mother? Did Lynn think that she was Kayla's example for her angry behavior?

Kayla walked over to her mother, looking her straight in the eyes. "Mom, you said you wanted things to change so you came to this class. I didn't tell them that you were the reason I was here. You owe it to me and yourself."

She turns and walks out of the room toward the exit doors. Kayla climbs into the van, puts her seatbelt on and looks out the window.

"Kayla, is your mother coming?" Lynn asks.

"Yes, she just had to use the bathroom," Kayla replied, hoping her mother wouldn't change her mind.

"Just a few more minutes and we'll be ready to go," Lynn announced as she notes everyone is on the van except Kayla's mother. She glances over at Kayla who is quietly staring out the window towards the exit doors. They slowly swing open as Valerie exits the building, hesitating briefly before boarding the van.

Kayla smiles, "Mom, I saved you a seat."

"Thanks," she replied slumping down in the seat next to her daughter.

"Where do you think we're going?" Kayla asks her mother. Mrs. Michaels doesn't answer as she silently wonders the same thing.

After a short ride to the city's south side, the van pulls up in front of a nursing home. It was called Promise Land Nursing Center, founded by Pastor Lee and local community leaders.

"Why are we at a nursing home?" Kayla asks with a puzzled look on her face.

"We are going to visit a young lady with a story to share about her relationship."

"Why did we come to her job? Couldn't she have just come to the community center?" Valerie questioned.

"No," Lynn replied with sternness in her tone.

As the group of women walk toward the building, Lynn

holds open the door smiling faintly. She leads them up

to the front desk and signs in.

"Hello Ms. Dean. I see you've brought visitors." The

nurse at the front desk smiles and passes out visitor

badges to everyone in the group.

"Yes, I have. We will be heading up now," she replies

as she pushes the button to the elevator.

They get on and stand in silence as the elevator slowly

jerks to a stop once it reaches the second floor.

"Here we are room 219," Lynn announces in a soft

voice.

One by one the women in the group slowly approach a

glass window. Behind the glass lies a young woman.

Her eyes are closed and a tube coming from her throat

is hooked up to a machine sitting beside the bed. She

lays motionless while a nurse checks her vital signs and replaces her IV bag.

The group looks at the young lady lying seemingly lifeless in the bed, wondering who she is and why a girl so young is in a nursing home. Kayla, sensing the questions no one else seemed to want to ask, speaks up. Placing her palms against the window, she asks Lynn, "Who is she and why is that tube in her throat? What happened to her?"

"This is my daughter Noelle. The tube is in her throat to help her breathe and she's here because her boyfriend beat her and left her for dead." Tears swell up in her eyes as Lynn answers Kayla's questions. Memories of Noelle's vibrant spirit and the light from her life that used to shine so brightly began to overwhelm her. That light had been snuffed leaving her daughter pale and lifeless. A small commotion behind her brings Lynn

back to herself. Turning around, she sees the young girl

Kayla running down the hallway in tears. Her mother

catchers her and wraps her in her arms to console her.

Wide eyed, the group looks back toward Lynn. Tina

stands by her side and puts a reassuring arm around

her waist. As Valerie and Kayla return to the window,

Lynn shares Noelle's story with the group. She holds a

picture of Noelle dressed in a volley ball uniform,

blonde shoulder length hair pulled back in a ponytail.

With bright blue eyes and a winning smile, she holds up

a trophy in triumphant poise.

"She met a young man named Will about six months

ago. He was a breath of fresh air for both of us, polite,

caring and generous with both his time and his money.

He possessed all of the qualities that her father did not,

or so I thought. His anger streak was subtle at first but I began to question her once she started coming home with bruises. She covered for him by saying it happened during volleyball practice. She had either run into one of the other players or she had fallen on the gym floor much too hard. Those were her excuses to me," Lynn pauses briefly. "I didn't say anything at first; I just paid closer attention to their interactions and declined his offers to dinner or to help around the house. I decided he couldn't use that any longer to win me over. I confronted her and pointed out all the red flags I could see to show her that I thought Will might be dangerous. She became upset and accused me of trying to ruin her life. She said, 'You didn't leave dad after all the times I begged you, so why should I listen to you now?' It hurt me to hear her say that and seeing her laying here now, I blame myself. If I had only left earlier she wouldn't have gotten the idea that it was okay to stay with someone who treated you badly." She wipes the tears from her eyes and continues, "Six weeks ago, I got a phone call from Will's dad telling me that the kids got into a fight and Will was going to jail. He said that Noelle was being flown by helicopter to Faith Clinic and I needed to get there right away. I don't know how I made it there other than by God's leading. As I rushed into the ER her friends Mya and Yvonna were talking with the police. They rushed over to me crying hysterically. The police officer took us into a private room to ask the girls some questions. According to her friends, Noelle came out of the Jones' house after telling Will that their relationship was over. He followed her outside and started arguing with her.

As she turned to walk away, he picked up a bat that was lying in the front yard and hit her in the back of the head. She fell instantly and he repeatedly swung the bat," Lynn takes a quick breath, "hitting my baby girl until she lay motionless on the ground, covered in blood. Mya and Yvonna got out of their car to help her and managed to finally grab the bat from out of his hands. With all the commotion going on, Mr. Jones came outside and then called for the police and paramedics. I applaud Mr. Jones for getting my daughter help as well as holding his son until the police arrived. When I first walked into her hospital room I didn't know who she was. Her head had swollen twice its size and her face was purple. Her eyes were swollen shut. I tried calling her name but she didn't respond. I was angry at myself, him, her and even God for letting this happen to my baby."

Lynn turns to the group looking at each one of them, gazing lastly upon Kayla, "You see, your actions do have a consequence and your parents and friends will do their best to help you. But if you don't listen then you will have to carry the weight of your decision. I want you all to remember that you do have a choice in your relationships. Never let someone tell you what you are. Know who you are and that God created you for a purpose. No one has the right to abuse or mistreat any of you physically or verbally. If you want out please contact the center, they have a 24-hour crisis line to assist you. Get out before it's too late." She turns back to the window to focus on her daughter.

"Ms. Dean, how long will Noelle be here?" Tina asked after a brief moment of silence.

Without turning she answers, "She may have suffered some brain damage. The doctor says it could be six months to a year but even then, she might not be able to live like a normal seventeen year-old. I have faith that the Lord will see her through."

Just then one of the nurses standing over to the side walks up to Lynn and places a hand on her shoulders.

"Good afternoon ladies, my name is Jene and I'm the head nurse for this floor. Every week Lynn arrives with a group of women, just like you, to show what can happen when you are in a relationship filled with domestic violence. I know that what you have seen and heard here today is quite upsetting but it is also very real. As one of the nurses here as well as a licensed counselor, I am here to answer any questions you may have before you leave. Is there anything any of you would like to ask me?"

The women all shake their heads no, too numb to speak.

The elevator door slides open as the van's driver, a young, Latino woman, steps onto the floor. Looking briefly over at Noelle, she turns toward Lynn and asks gently, "Are you ready to return to the center?"

She smiles and nods. "Maria will take you all back to the center," Lynn explains. "I am going to stay here with my daughter a little while longer. Remember what you've seen and heard here today. Remember Noelle's story. Thank you all for coming and sharing a part of your lives with the rest of us. There will be another session two weeks from now where we will discuss the laws pertaining to domestic violence and the resources available to you once you leave that situation."

One by one each member of the group hugs Lynn and gets on the elevator. As the doors close, Kayla looks over at her mother and notices a tear in her eye, something she hasn't seen since her father left.

"Mom, what's wrong?"

"I realized by seeing that girl lying in that bed that if I don't learn to control my anger I could hurt you." She hugs Kayla and as the doors slide open, they both step off of the elevator together.

The ride back to the community center is long and silent. "Man, Lynn is strong," Tina remarks in an attempt to break the silence. "I don't know if I could handle what she's going through. I got some brothers that would've beaten that boy down." Adjusting the passenger side window Tina continues, "I'm glad I'm in this class. The more I think about her daughter the madder I get." Turning to Maria she asks, "Ms. Maria, do you know what happened to that boy?"

"He is in jail and will be for at least 25 years, with no chance for parole. He was charged with attempted murder."

"I hope the Lord forgives him." Tina remarks sarcastically.

As the van pulls into the parking lot Kayla can't believe her eyes. She spots Mark among a small group of teenage boys waiting to load another passenger van. Mark quickly looks away after making eye contact with her.

"Come on Kayla, it's time to go," her mother calls.

She walks into the center and signs out. Curious as to why Mark is there, she looks at the sign-in sheet but doesn't see his name. Disappointed, she leaves and gets into her mother's car.

CHAPTER FIVE

"Why am I here?" Mark asked defiantly getting into the van. He was slightly irritated after spotting Kayla at the center.

"You are here to find out what domestic violence is about and the consequences of your actions if you continue on the wrong path," Mr. Anderson replied. He was the director and group leader at the Family Life Community Center.

"What if you didn't do nothing and she just went off on you? Don't you have the right to defend yourself?"

"There is a way to defend yourself without using violence."

"I got to see this," replies Mark with a smirk.

"Remember gentlemen on this trip you will see and hear things that are quite disturbing. Just know if you don't heed the advice given to you today, you might not get a second chance."

The ride from the center to the correctional facility was an hour long. Mark kept to himself as the other young boys talked nervously about what to expect once they arrived. Mr. Anderson listened in silence. Prison life was not the life portrayed in music videos as these young boys would soon find out. As the van pulled up in front of the county correctional facility, they were met by two armed guards.

"Why we got to come here and learn about domestic violence? Couldn't we learn about this stuff back at the community center?" Mark questioned.

Mr. Anderson addressed Mark's remarks after locking the van doors. "Mark, there are lessons to be learned outside of the classroom too. Sometimes you learn more after having experienced the reality of things."

They are escorted into a holding area where another set of guards are waiting. Everyone is searched and told to leave their personal belongings behind in a locker.

"I feel naked without my stuff," Chad, a boy slightly taller than Mark gripes as he takes off his jewelry. Next they enter into a large meeting area where they are greeted by Mr. Jameson, the facility instructor, and four inmates sitting behind a long table. Two of them looked much younger than Mark while the other two seemed just slightly older.

"Have a seat gentlemen. I'm Mr. Jameson, a life coach and one of the instructors here at the county correctional facility. You will hear from a couple of young men, some your age and older, who are here to share how their negative decisions got them here. We will start with you." He points to one of the young inmates sitting to his left.

"My name is Jason. I'm 17 and I am here because I robbed a store. I got 15 years for it."

"I've been in trouble before and the judge told me if I came back in there, I was going to regret it. He was right…I hate being in here not being able to see my family or friends."

He lowers his head as the young man next to him begins to speak.

"My name is Big Rick and I'm 18 years old. I was in the drug game and got caught. I got 20 years. I used to make drug runs and even recruited some younger kids to help me sell it. I didn't know the police had been watchin' me for a year and set me up. Now I'm locked up."

"My name is Luke, I'm 21 and I used to run women. You know, they made money for me." He chuckled slightly at the embarrassed looks on the young boy's faces. "I might be here for 10 to 15 years. I recruited girls that didn't have many friends or self-worth. I would take them out, make them feel wanted and then turn them out to the streets. The judge said I was a predator and after I serve me sentence, I will have to register as a sex offender for life. Take it from me, learn from us and change before it's too late."

"My name is Will Jones. I'm 19 and I'm here because I beat my girlfriend in the head with a bat and she almost died. They charged me with attempted murder and I got 25 years. If she dies, I could be charged with murder and spend the rest of my life behind bars. My dad is so mad at me that he doesn't even come to see me."

Mark looks at Will, stunned by what he just heard, and raises his hand to ask a question.

"Yes Mark?"

Looking at Will in disbelief, "You have to be lying. Man what were you thinkin?"

"I just got mad," Will answered leaning back nonchalantly. "She said she didn't want to be with me no more so I wanted to make sure she wasn't going to be with someone else. I didn't mean to hit her so hard; I just lost it I guess."

"What did you think hittin her in the head was going to do? Make her want you more?" Mark asked.

The other inmates chuckle softly as Mr. Anderson tries to get Mark's attention.

"And I guess you're here because you did everything right in your relationship?" Will snapped. "Man shut up if all you are here to do is judge me. I'm trying to help you out."

"He's right," Mr. Jameson interjected, interrupting the two of them. "Young man, the purpose of this visit is to show you what can happen if you don't change your ways. In here you don't get to hang out with your friends, chase girls and listen to music. You do as you are told, which means you get up, get dressed, eat, go to school and see your family when they say you can. There is a price to pay for not following the rules."

"Pointing out his wrong doesn't excuse you from what you have done, or you wouldn't be in this group today," Mr. Anderson adds after Mr. Jameson finishes speaking.

Mark slumps down in his chair and crosses his arms in defiance. Terry, one of the other boys in the group, pokes him in the arm. Mark ignores him, embarrassed that he had to be corrected in front of everyone.

"Who made you come here anyway?" Will questioned him.

"My principal sent me."

"Oh, so you was acting up in school, bad move man. Without an education you don't have nothin."

"No I get pretty good grades. I'm just a ladies' man and she couldn't handle it. She went and attacked me from behind and I threw her off of me, so the principal said I had to come to this meeting."

"A girl is not going to attack you just because you got another girl," Luke jumps in.

"I was running women left and right. Yeah, some of them were jealous but they kept it between them and not me. Did you hit her?"

Apprehensively, Mark answered, "I didn't hit her. I just pushed her into a locker and spit in her face."

"So see you're just like me," Will sneered. "You sit there judging me and beat up on your girl too. Ain't that something?"

"You ain't nothing but a little punk hittin on girls," Big Rick chimed in.

"Well at least I didn't hit my girl with no bat. Besides, she wasn't even hurt. She said she was going to find someone else so I had to set her straight." Putting his hand on his chin with his head cocked slightly to the side, "She wasn't going to play a playa. This man don't get played."

"Do you know how dumb you sound? You're probably only what, fifteen?"

"Yeah."

"You'd better listen or you're going to join us. I hit my girl because I thought I could control her. She would always be there for me but now look at me. I'm here doing what they tell me to do," he points toward Mr. Jameson and the guards. "It's only been six weeks but I got 25 years here. I know I messed up and I'm trying to do right."

Mr. Anderson asks the panel of men to tell the group what led them to their decisions and if they would now do things differently.

"I wouldn't listen to all those people telling me it was easy to just take what I wanted and run. The same people that told me to do that are the same ones that left me to get caught," Jason replied.

"I grew up in the hood. Everyone was dealin' so I thought that was my only choice. My mom told me I could be different, but I just didn't listen," replied Big Rick.

"Listening to music and watching videos. Seeing how they lived, I wanted to do it too. I'm learning now to be a leader not a follower," says Luke.

"I guess I was mad because my mom left me. I felt rejected and I thought I really did love Noelle. She was pretty and smart. I bought her anything she wanted to show her I loved her. I guess it wasn't enough. I'm learning now how to deal with my feelings and not to let them get the best of me," Will replied.

"Let's give these young men a hand," Mark says sarcastically, standing and clapping his hands.

"Sit down," Mr. Anderson ordered Mark. "Your lack of respect shown here today tells me why you needed to be here. I have to give a report to your principal so if I were you, I'd act like I wanted to go back to Virtue Christian Academy."

"I don't care about that school," Mark replied sitting down slightly embarrassed.

Will just shakes his head. Looking over at Luke and Mr. Jameson he nods his head as if he were in agreement with them in something. Will gets up and starts toward the door, Luke follows. Without a word they turn and grab Mark, dragging him out of his chair and pinning him against the wall. With eyes as big as tea cups Mark

tries with everything he has to get away.

"How does it feel now to have someone put their hands

on you?" Luke asks.

"I don't hear you man, what did you say?"

"Alright you two, put him down and go back to your

room." As the guards approach Luke and Will, Mr.

Jameson adds, "You know the rules, no putting your

hands on the visitors."

Letting him go, Mark falls to the floor. Luke and Will

high five each other and wait as the guards chain their

wrists and ankles before escorting them back to their

cell. Looking at the smiling faces of the other inmates,

Mark sits down too upset to speak.

"Well, I hope all of you learned something here today

that will help you make better decisions in your life. I

hope to never see you in here. Enjoy your day and your freedom."

Mr. Jameson shakes hands with Mr. Anderson and shackles Big Rick and Jason.

"Bye Mark," they say in a soft voice, laughing so hard they can barely walk.

The young men in Mark's group start in on him too.

"You need a guard to walk you to the van?" Terry asks.

Everyone laughs as Mark takes a step toward Terry.

"All of you can…." Mark begins.

"Watch yourself Mark!" Mr. Anderson warns, stepping in between Mark and the rest of the group. "I don't think you want to spend the night here."

The doors clang shut behind Jason and Big Rick as they shuffle down the hallway. The guards escort the group back to the waiting area to collect their things. Outside in the van, Chad puts his jewelry back on and takes his seat. Mark quietly takes a seat in the back of the van as they head back to the community center.

Mr. Anderson makes his way toward Mark to address his behavior, while the rest of the group sits up front discussing what they'd just seen. Sitting down across the aisle from Mark he asks, "Did you get anything out of this visit today?"

"Yes," Mark replies staring blankly out the window.

"What was that?"

"Beating up people is only cool if you don't get caught."

"Are you serious?"

Mark looks over at Mr. Anderson not saying a word and turns to look again out the window.

"I hope you grow up young man and start to take life seriously." Mr. Anderson goes back to the front of the van and continues his discussion with Terry and Chad. Mark watches them talk while he thinks about what Will said concerning his relationship with Noelle. Could he really hit a girl with a bat? He had never been that mad and didn't think he could ever go there. He thought about what it would mean to lose his freedom and having to deal with people like Luke and Big Rick. "Uh Mr. Anderson, can I talk to you?" Mark asks. Mr. Anderson was in the middle of finishing notes when he paused, looking up at Mark in surprise. He slowly closes his notebook and moves to the back.

CHAPTER SIX

Sitting down beside Mark, he patiently waits to hear what the young man has to say.

"I know my attitude hasn't been right on this trip, I'm just tired of people comin' at me like I'm some woman beater. That ain't even me."

"So how are you going to change to show others you are not some woman beater?"

"I don't know," Mark sighed. "What do you think I should do?"

"Come to the community center for some classes to explain domestic violence and the impact that it has on you and your partner. I'll also set aside some counseling time to address the source of your anger.

There are more positive ways for young men to handle their emotions and I will show you."

"Alright, but you better not try to make me cry or talk crazy to me like they do on those stupid talk shows."

Laughing, Mr. Anderson agrees but only on the grounds that Mark does not waste his time. He has to take these sessions seriously. As the van pulls back into the community center parking lot, everyone gets out.

"Mark," Terry calls after him.

"What's up?"

"Hey man, I hope you get it together. I don't think you would do well in the county jail."

"I hear you man," he replies with a small laugh.

They exchange a handshake and Terry walks into the center.

"You can come Monday after school Mark and we can talk then." Mr. Anderson hands Mark a permission slip for his parents to sign.

"Okay Mr. Anderson. I can use this as proof to show my parents that I do want to better my attitude and my behavior." Mark shoves the permission slip in his back pocket. "They don't think that I can change."

"Well if you acted at home like you did this morning, I can't fault them for that." Mr. Anderson extends his hand out toward Mark, "We can't make you change. You have to want to do it for yourself."

Mark nods as he shakes Mr. Anderson's hand and walks away.

Starting home, Mark considers changing his ways. He wondered if things would get better for him if he did. As he inserts his key to unlock the door, he walks in to see a box with a 'for sale' sign attached to it. Looking

inside, he's surprised to see his CD player, all of his

CDs, his Xbox and the games that came with it.

Another box holding his TV was off to the side.

Instantly, all thoughts of changing for the better vanish.

"MOM!" he yells.

Mr. Parks slowly walks out of the family room.

Lowering his voice, Mark demands, "Dad, why are you

selling my stuff?"

"Sit down Mark," Mr. Parks replies gently.

Both of them sit down on opposite sides of the room.

"Your mother and I talked last night and we both

decided to take away those things that we feel have a

negative impact on your behavior."

"It's just music dad. Besides, you don't have to sell

them all do you?"

"That's going to be up to you. If your behavior improves then you can earn your belongings back. The CDs however are most definitely going."

Stunned by his parents' decision, Mark heads upstairs toward his room. A sudden thought crosses his mind and he heads down the hall to his parents' bedroom instead. Within minutes he comes down the stairs carrying a box full of his parents' valuable possessions.

"Hey Mom, how much do you think I can get for this Coach purse?" he asks. "Dad, how much would your laptop and cufflinks sell for?"

Turning around, they are shocked by their son's outright disregard of their parental authority and lack of respect for their personal belongings.

"I don't believe you Mark," his mom shakes her head in disbelief.

"Believe it baby. An eye for an eye," Mark replies looking defiantly from one parent to the other.

"If you don't put my things back you won't have any eyes," his dad snaps glaring angrily at his son.

Despite seeing his father's nostrils flaring and veins straining in his face, Mark asks, "Well, are you going to put my stuff back?"

"Shelly, call the police..."

"What, why?" Mrs. Parks looks over at her husband confused by his request.

"Because your son and I are about to go to jail." Mr. Parks takes a step toward Mark.

Realizing that he may have overstepped the line, Mark slowly places the box down on the floor. "Sike Mom, I was just playin'. Dad, why are you so serious?"

"Get out of this house!" Mr. Parks replies without blinking an eye. "And don't come back until you can respect us."

Looking stunned, Mark walks through the kitchen and out the back door.

"Michael, you can't just leave him out there. What is he supposed to do? Where is he going to go?"

"I don't know and I honestly don't care at this moment. He is not going to stand in my face and disrespect me in my own house!"

Grabbing his car keys, Mr. Parks heads for the door.

"Where are you going?" Mrs. Parks asks.

"I'm going to talk to Mr. Anderson and see what went on today. Something has happened that caused Mark to lose his mind." Looking at his wife, Mr. Parks pleads,

"Do not let him back in this house until we all sit down and talk."

Backing down the driveway, Mr. Parks fumes as he thinks about Mark and how disrespectful he has become in the past couple of months. "Every since we got saved," he thought, "Shelly and I have gotten better but Mark's attitude has gotten worse."

Pulling into the parking lot of the community center, Mr. Parks spots Mr. Anderson heading for his car.

"Mr. Anderson!"

Slow turning around, not recognizing the man walking toward him, he cautiously replies, "Yes, can I help you?"

"My name is Michael Parks. I'm Mark Parks' father."

Softening his stance, Mr. Anderson responds, "How can I help you Mr. Parks? Did Mark tell you about his trip to the county correctional facility?"

"No, that's what I've come to talk to you about. He came back worse than when he'd left."

Looking confused Mr. Anderson replied, "What do you mean? I spoke to him before he left and he shared with me his desire to change. We agreed that he would come to the center and learn about domestic violence and how to use more positive ways to express his emotions. He was supposed to give you a permission slip to attend our first counseling session on Monday."

"Oh really? He didn't share any of that with us."

Taking a deep breath, Mr. Parks proceeded to tell Mr. Anderson about what happened the night the school principal paid them a visit. He shared how he and his wife made the decision to sell some of Mark's things

that they believed contributed to his negative behavior.

"We were going to sell his CD player and his music,"

Mr. Parks continued. "The Xbox and TV would be

returned once he changed his behavior but we didn't

get a chance to discuss that point in detail. Instead he

went into our room, returning with a box of my things

and things of my wife's. After asking us what we

thought he could get from selling our stuff, I told him to

put our things down and to get out of my house. How

was his behavior during the trip? Did he cooperate or

did he give you an attitude?"

"Mark was not cooperative at first and I told him that I

would have to let his principal know about his

behavior," explained Mr. Anderson. "He said he didn't

care about that school, but you and your wife wanted him to go there."

"He's right. I was hoping his first year in a Christian school would be a positive experience for him. Unfortunately, he acts worse now than he did before he started going. We try to do right. We take him to church with us each week but he continually acts out in a negative manner."

"You have to understand Mr. Parks that you can only show your child by example how to live. They have to make the final decisions for themselves. And as a man of God, you can only live a Godly lifestyle, not only before your son but for everyone that you may meet. We can't force God on anyone," Mr. Anderson smiles reassuringly, "just pray that he will take heed and come around."

"I don't know man...I was ready to knock that joker out," Mr. Parks responded, throwing jabs in the air like a boxer.

"Remember Mr. Parks, kids live what they learn. I'll be sure to follow up with Mr. Chase on Monday to arrange transportation from school over to the center."

"Thanks Mr. Anderson."

As the two shake hands and turn to leave, four masked males approach them from behind.

"Gimme what you got and nobody gets hurt," one of them growled.

"You young punks better get out of here. You're in the wrong area to be playing games," Mr. Anderson replied calmly as he stepped toward the group. They take off running down the alleyway behind the center. Quite shaken and puzzled, Mr. Parks asks Mr. Anderson,

"How did you know that those boys would not attack us? What if one of them had pulled out a weapon?"

"I've been working at the community center far too long. If anyone in this neighborhood is bold enough to approach me, they know that they'd better have a gun."

Mr. Anderson surveys the scene for a moment before focusing back on Mr. Parks. "Are you okay?"

"Yeah, just a little shaken," Mr. Parks replies.

Walking him over to his car, Mr. Anderson comments on Mr. Parks' decision to sell some of Mark's things. "I think that it was a good idea to give Mark an ultimatum and to sell his music. Too many of our young boys are influenced by the rappers in music videos and how they treat the females like property. Some of the lyrics are very crude and I have to correct the young boys here at the center daily to treat the young girls with respect."

As he shuts his door, Mr. Parks nods his head in agreement and drives off. After a few blocks, he lays his head back on the headrest, looks upward and says, "Thank you Lord for looking out for me." Breathing a sigh of relief, he approaches a stoplight and slows to a halt. Turning to his right, he notices four young men laughing as they walk down the street. Looking more closely, he realizes that they have on the same clothes as the males who had approached him and Mr. Anderson back at the community center. Reaching for his cell phone to call the police, he suddenly freezes in horror as one of the young men stoops to pick something up from the ground.

"Mark! Mark!"

Turning around, Mark realizes that it's his dad calling him and takes off running down the street and around the corner. The group of boys with him take off running as well.

"Man why you runnin'? Who is that, the police?" asks Louis, one of the boys running behind him.

"No man, that's my dad."

"What! Man we was about to rob your dad, are you crazy?" Louis stops running and speaks to Joe-Joe and Chris. "This fool was about to have us caught up in some craziness," Louis growls while pointing a finger toward Mark. "We were already taking a chance trying to rob Mr. Anderson but that other guy...man that was his dad!"

"I promise I didn't know it was him until he turned around. What was I supposed to do, tell you that he's my dad so leave him alone?" Mark shrugged his shoulders, "Besides, I'm mad at him anyway."

Joe-Joe and Chris roll their eyes in disgust and look at Louis. Shaking his head, Louis speaks to Mark, "Man you are lame. We're done with you, go home. The streets ain't for you." Laughing they turn to walk away. "Forget you Louis, you a fake gangsta anyway." As Mark turns away, he's grabbed from behind and thrown to the ground. Louis, Joe-Joe and Chris start punching, kicking and stomping on Mark as he desperately tries covering his face from the heavy blows. As a car screeches to a halt, Louis and the other boys turn and run away, leaving Mark on the ground badly bruised and bleeding from his mouth and nose. Mr. Parks jumps out of his car and runs over to his son. "Mark! Mark!" Mr. Parks yells as he falls on his knees beside his son.

"Dad, I think I'm going to die," Mark replies in a weak voice. He turns on his side to spit out more blood and closes his eyes.

"No son, I got you." Mr. Parks slowly picks Mark up from the ground and runs to his car. Gently laying Mark down in the backseat, he races to the nearest emergency room which happens to be Faith Clinic. Pulling into the parking lot, Mr. Parks wildly bears down on the horn. He jumps out of the car and opens the back door to get Mark out. Two attendants rush out of the lobby doors, placing Mark in a wheelchair to rush him inside for treatment.

"What happened sir?" a nurse asks as she applies pressure to stop the blood flow from the back of Mark's head.

"My son, my son was attacked," Mr. Parks replies trying to gain his composure.

"Stay calm sir, we are going to take him back to the ER right now." As the nurse pushes his son through the double doors to the ER, Mr. Parks fumbles with his wallet to get his medical card. His hands are shaking as he reaches down to pick up his cell phone that had fallen to the floor in the midst of all of the commotion. moments later a doctor in scrubs comes through the double doors and walks toward Mr. Parks. Rushing toward him, Mr. Parks blurts out, "My name is Mr. Parks and that's my son Mark…"

"Mr. Parks, my name is Dr. Wood. I was finishing up with another patient when they brought your son in. It appears that he may have suffered some broken bones and there may be internal injuries," Dr. Wood pauses briefly and lays a hand on Mr. Park's shoulders. "We are going to take some x-rays just to be sure. I promise you that we will do all that we can to take care of Mark." As. Dr. Wood hands a chart over to the nurse at the front desk, Mr. Parks finds a chair in the waiting room and sits down. He dials unsuccessfully to reach his wife because his hands won't stop shaking. Holding his right arm steady, he clutches the phone and raises it to his ear.

"Hello?"

"Shelly, you need to get to Faith Clinic now!"

"What's happened Michael? Where is Mark?"

"We're in the ER. Just get here and I'll tell you….hello? Shelly?"

The phone somehow disconnects and he calls back a second time. The phone just rings and when he calls for a third time, it goes straight to voicemail. He hangs up in frustration. The lobby doors swing open a few minutes later as Mrs. Parks comes running toward her husband.

"What happened?" she asks with fear in her eyes.

"Mark was jumped by a group of young boys. They beat him pretty bad Shelly...the doctor said he may have some broken bones and other internal injuries. They took some x-rays and someone should be updating us with those test results soon. I got to him as soon as I could Shelly," Mr. Parks exclaims with tears in his eyes.

Mrs. Parks sits down and looks at her husband. "This wouldn't have happened if you didn't put him out," she replied slowly, trying to remain calm.

"No Shelly, this wouldn't have happened if Mark hadn't tried to rob me and Mr. Anderson at the community center."

"What are you saying Michael?"

Taking her by the hand, Mr. Parks explains, "Our son and some thugs tried to rob me at the community center. I guess he ran when he realized that it was me."

Leaning on her husband, Mrs. Parks begins to weep.

A police officer slowly walks over to them.

"Mr. and Mrs. Parks," he asks softly.

"Yes?"

"I'm Officer Davenport and I was told that your son was assaulted. I just wanted to know from you if this was related to an attempted robbery at the community center. Mr. Anderson made a report that…"

"Right now is not a good time Officer Davenport," Mr.

Parks interrupts, "the doctor is checking Mark out now

and we are waiting for an update. I don't know what's

goin on. I just know three young punks jumped my

son. I really can't focus enough to tell you what

happened. Do you have a card or something so that I

can contact you later?"

"Yes I do," he replies pulling a card from his back

pocket. "I understand that this is a difficult time for you

and your wife. Please contact me as soon as you can.

The quicker we get the information out, the sooner we

can catch those responsible for this awful attack on your

son."

"I appreciate that. We will be in touch."

As they watch Officer Davenport walk away, Mrs.

Parks turns to her husband, "Let's pray Michael."

The Parks hold hands and ask God to forgive them of any sins and to heal their relationship with their son. They pray for Mark to come through his surgery alright. As they finish praying a nurse enters the waiting room and looks around. "Mr. Parks?" she asks as she walks toward them slowly. "Dr. Wood wanted to let you know that your son will be just fine. There were a few broken bones but no internal injuries."

"Thank you." Mr. Parks smiles as he hugs his wife.

"God does answer prayers," the nurse replied as she walked out of the room.

Hours seem to pass before they hear from Dr. Wood. "There was no internal bleeding but he did suffer a few cracked ribs, a broken wrist and a fractured jaw. We had to put a cast on his arm and bandaged his ribs. We've wired his jaws to keep them shut. His mouth will have to remain closed for a few weeks in order for his jaw to heal properly." Smiling reassuringly Dr. Wood continues, "He's still heavily sedated but I'll take you to his room so you can see him."

They follow Dr. Wood down the hallway to Mark's room. Mr. Parks pushes the door open slowly, now knowing what to expect. Mark is lying in bed with his eyes closed. His head is wrapped up in one huge bandage. His arm lies at his side with a cast up to his elbow.

"This will prevent Mark from bending his wrist so it can heal," Dr. Wood explains.

With tears in her eyes, Mrs. Parks rushes to her son's side. "My baby, you're going to be alright," she cries holding his hand.

Thanking Dr. Wood, Mr. Parks slowly makes his way over to his son. Thoughts of the past few days play in his mind as he sits by the bed. "I don't know where we went wrong but I pray that this will open your eyes and that you will want to change."

The door opens as a nurse walks in to check on Mark. "Mr. and Mrs. Parks, my name is Carrie. I'll be the nurse for this shift," she explained. "It's after 6 o'clock and the cafeteria will be closing in an hour. If you want a bite to eat, you will need to get something now or you'll have to wait until it opens again Sunday morning around 6 am."

"Thank you," Mrs. Parks replies barely above a whisper as Carrie finishes her check-list and leaves the room. "You go on home Mike, I'll stay here tonight."

"No," Mr. Parks lifts his head from his hands, "I want us both to be here when he wakes up."

Later that evening, Mark begins to move and groans loudly in pain. Realizing that he can't open his mouth, he opens his eyes in a panic. Mrs. Parks holds Mark's hand to reassure him. "It's okay Mark, your jaw is wired shut. You can't open your mouth right now," his mom tells him gently rubbing his hand.

He looks at her with tears in his eyes. He remembers leaving home and hangin' out with Louis and his boys. As his father leans over the bed, he remembers the rest and looks away ashamed.

"Son, we're going to find out who did this to you but right now, you just rest." Mr. Parks smiles lovingly at his son. His heart breaks in silence as Mark begins to cry.

CHAPTER SEVEN

The following Sunday morning, Kayla and her mother are preparing for Sunday school.

"Kayla, are you ready?" Mrs. Michaels calls as she heads toward the front door.

"I'm fixin' my hair Mom; I'll be down in a minute." As she uses her flat iron to straighten her bangs, Kayla lays it down on her dresser and turns it off. Grabbing her comb and brush, she looks at her father's face down picture and picks it back up. Kneeling beside her bed, Kayla reflects back to Friday and all the things that had taken place. Taking a deep breath, she says a quick prayer, *"Okay God, I hope you still remember me, it's Kayla Michaels. I'm going to your house today. I have messed up these past few months and even the last few days. I pray that you will forgive me and let me hear from you about what I*

need to do. Amen."

Leaving her bedroom and running downstairs, Kayla

grabs her jacket and keys. She locks the door behind

her and gets in the car as her mother patiently waits.

"Did you want to talk to Pastor Lee today?" she asks

while backing out of the driveway.

"Sure Mom," she responds, surprised by her mother's

question. "Are you going to talk?"

"Yes. I feel that it's time to be open and tell what's on

my heart."

Kayla smiles and turns to look out the window. As they

pull into the church parking lot, Kayla sees Mya and

D'nea talking.

"Give me a few minutes Mom."

"Okay, but don't be long. Sunday school starts in fifteen minutes."

As Mrs. Michaels goes into the church, Kayla walks over to the two girls. They are standing beside a new Lexus GS and appear to be in deep conversation about something.

"Nice car Mya."

"Thanks Kayla." They hug and slowly walk over toward the steps leading inside.

"Hey Kayla, how are you?" D'nea asks.

"I'm good, tryin' to get back on track."

"Do you know some boy from your school named Mark Parks?"

Looking at D'nea confused as to why she asked about Mark she answers, "Yeah I know him why?"

"I heard he got beat up pretty bad yesterday."

"That's what he gets," she replies smiling deviously.

"I'm serious Kayla, he's in the hospital. He had to get his jaw wired shut," D'nea replies in a somber tone.

"Wow, I didn't think it was *that* bad. I thought you meant he got into a fight and got beat up. Does anyone know what happened?" Kayla asks with a bit of conviction in her voice.

"I guess he got jumped. I don't know the whole story. Why would you say that's what he gets?" D'nea questions her.

"We broke up last week and he acts like he's God's gift to women. He actually spit in my face and pushed me into a locker, so I was just saying maybe he deserved to get beat up but not like that. Now I feel bad."

"Don't Kayla," Mya says putting an arm across her shoulder. "It's not your fault Mark got beat up. All you can do is pray that he will recover."

"I guess you're right."

They walk into the church and down the hall to the youth department's classroom.

"Good morning Miss Kayla," Pastor Charles greeted her.

"Hi Pastor Charles."

"Good to see you for service."

"I'm glad to be here," she replies smiling.

"Let us start class with prayer."

Pastor Charles leads the Sunday school in prayer. They spend the next hour discussing the scripture reading for that day. After Sunday school is over, Mya tells Kayla about upcoming events at the church.

"Hey Kayla, you know we are having Friends and Family Day in three weeks. The youth department is going to do a dance and a skit. You want to be a part of it?"

"I don't know...my mom works crazy hours so I don't know how I would get here. And I haven't been here in a long time. Let me speak with Pastor Charles and Pastor Lee about it."

"I told you before that I could come pick you up." Mya responds while placing her hands on her hips.

"I'll let you know Mya, I promise."

As the students put away their Bibles, they head down the hallway toward the sanctuary. Kayla reminisces on how she used to be a part of the dance team and how much she enjoyed ministering before the Lord. She felt free, like there was no else but her and God in the room.

It made her smile to know that she was doing something that pleased God. As she enters into the sanctuary her mother stops her.

"Kayla, come here."

She anxiously walks over to her mother as she sees the look of concern on her face.

"Yes Mom?"

"I just heard about Mark. Do you know what happened?"

Kayla shakes her head no. "All I know is what Mya and D'nea told me before Sunday school."

Putting an arm around her daughter, Mrs. Michaels makes a small request, "I know this may sound strange but you make sure you pray for him."

"Yes Mom."

She turns and walks to her seat. The musicians are playing quietly as the sanctuary begins to fill. Members from other Bible classes as well as those who are just arriving, greet one another warmly as they take to their seats. The call for prayer is announced and people go up to the altar to pray. As Kayla kneels down to pray, she thinks about all of the changes she has had to endure the past six months. Her father leaves, forcing her mother to work two jobs just to make ends meet. The many times her mom came home angry and abusive; the emotional roller coaster ride with Mark. Tears slowly fall down her cheeks.

"God, please forgive me. Help me, make me better."

As she finishes her prayer, Kayla grabs a tissue to dry her eyes. As she walks back to her seat she sees Pastor

Lee standing in the back of the sanctuary. She walks up to him, still somber from her prayer.

"Welcome back Kayla," he says and gives her a hug.

She begins to cry again, feeling overwhelmed by the love she has been shown this morning.

"I'll see you after service."

"Okay," she takes her seat and he heads down the aisle to the pulpit.

Pastor Lee speaks on the topic of forgiveness. "Forgive others for the way they have treated you. Forgive them for the things they have spoken about you. Forgive them even for all of the wrong they may have done toward you..."

Kayla and Valerie look at one another.

Valerie whispers to her, "Will you forgive me?"

Kayla smiles and whispers back, "Yes."

At the end of service, Kayla meets Mya in the

fellowship hall.

"So you think you will dance with us?" Mya asks still

pestering Kayla.

"I'm not sure, let me text you later."

"Okay Kayla," Mya walks down the steps and out the

door.

"Are you ready Kayla?" Sister Lee asks as she and Mrs.

Michaels stand in the doorway of the sanctuary.

"Yes I'm ready."

They walk over to Pastor Lee's office.

"Good afternoon everyone."

"Good afternoon Pastor Lee," Valerie responds.

"So how are things going with you and Kayla?"

"Kayla and I have spent some time together this

weekend and have had a chance to review what's been

happening in our lives. I guess I was angry after my husband left without any explanation. I felt that if I could keep Kayla under control then everything else would be okay. I didn't know how much the separation actually affected her and I realized that I never took the time to find out. After attending the domestic violence session and visiting Lynn's daughter at the nursing home, I recognized that I needed to let go of my anger or I could really hurt Kayla."

"I'm glad you were able to admit that you had a problem and that you are willing to work to make your relationship better with your daughter. Kayla how do you feel about what your mom has said?" Pastor Lee asked.

"She's always been so strong. After Dad left, she just took on more hours at work and moved on. She showed no emotion so I didn't think him leaving affected her all that much. I'm glad she can talk to me now without getting angry or hitting me. I was coming to a point where I couldn't take it anymore, and I was prepared to fight her back if necessary."

With an amazed look on her face Sister Lee asked, "Do you think that would have solved anything?"

"Not really but I wanted her to know I was tired of her hitting me."

"Valerie, I would like for you to attend some classes for adult women here at the church every Wednesday."

Sister Lee looked at the church calendar hanging on the wall, "Do you think you would be able to be here around 6 o'clock?"

"I might be able to."

Pastor Lee turns to Kayla. "I want you to continue working with the youth department. The young people will be performing for our Friends and Family Day service in three weeks. I think it would be good for you to be a part of it."

"Did Mya talk to you about me?" she asked.

"No, I just felt it would be a good thing for you to participate in."

"Okay," she smiled.

"Let's meet again next Sunday to see how things are going. What do you say?" Pastor Lee stands and shakes hands with Kayla and her mother.

"Sounds good to me," Kayla replied.

"We'll be here," Valerie says as she gathers her things and heads toward the door.

Kayla and her mother leave the church arm in arm,

smiling.

CHAPTER EIGHT

In the car Kayla and Valerie talk about Sunday's service and the changes they plan on making in their lives. As they pull out of the drive thru after ordering some food, Kayla shares her thoughts about forgiveness.

"I want to be forgiving but it's hard. Sometimes it's easier to be mad," Kayla says picking the onions off of her sandwich.

"I know but look what happens to you when you don't forgive," Mrs. Michaels responds while popping an onion ring in her mouth.

"I guess it's a day to day thing." Kayla lets out a sigh and starts eating her sandwich.

"Speaking of forgiveness, you can start by forgiving Mark. He could really use a friend right now."

"I know Mom, but just let me deal with him when I'm ready."

"Okay."

They pull into their driveway. Kayla grabs her purse and goes into the house. Mrs. Michaels pauses on the porch to pick up the newspaper as Kayla sits down at the kitchen table and finishes her lunch. As her mother gets things out of the freezer to prepare for dinner, Kayla throws her trash away. Walking toward the kitchen door, she stops suddenly turning to look at her mother.

"Mom, do you still love dad?"

Surprised by the question, Valerie replies, "Yes Kayla. I do and will probably always care for him."

"Do you ever wonder how he could say he loved you and then leave you?" Kayla asks cautiously, not wanting to make her mom upset.

"I used to but now I just trust that God knows what's best for me. Now go on upstairs and change your clothes. It's going to be a few hours before the roast is done."

As she turns and walks upstairs, Kayla takes out her phone and sends a text message to Mya.

"When iz practze?"

"Weds @ 6:30pm."

"Ok."

Monday morning arrives and the hallways of Virtue Christian Academy are once again buzzing with news. The students are discussing the weekend jumping of

Mark by a group of thugs. Casey and Brianna wait for Kayla at her locker.

"What's up ladies...?" Kayla glides down the hallway, hair tied back with a navy blue and gold head band.

"So you know right?" Brianna blurts out.

"Know what?" Kayla replied looking confused.

"About Mark," Casey hesitates. "He was..."

"Oh, yeah, I heard about that yesterday at church."

"Church?" Brianna starts with a laugh.

"Yes, I went to church yesterday." Kayla playfully pokes her friend in the arm.

"Wow, prayers do get answered," Casey replied sarcastically.

"After last week I knew I needed to do something," Kayla replied ignoring her friend's remark. "Me and moms was going at it and I just couldn't take it anymore. We went to church Friday night and I talked with my pastor and Pastor Charles. You know the one over the youth department."

Brianna and Casey both nod their heads.

"I had to go to some group about domestic violence. It was crazy. We ended up at this nursing home and there was a girl there our age. Her boyfriend hit her in the head with a bat and now she may be brain dead. She lies there unconscious with a tube in her throat to help her breathe. That freaked me out. Her life will never be the same and her boyfriend is in jail charged with attempted murder." Kayla holds her hands up, "I learned my lesson about putting my hands on folks just because I'm angry. Now that don't mean I won't defend myself if I have too, but I won't do it just trying to make my point."

"Wow Kayla, it sounds like you did have an interesting weekend," Brianna said with a grin.

"Miracles do come true," Casey followed laughing.

"So are you going to see Mark? I heard he's messed up pretty bad." Brianna asks while looking over her homework assignment.

"Bri-Bri, he's not my man anymore. I hope he's okay but I'm not going up there to see him."

"Kayla, I thought you loved him?" Brianna questioned while putting her notebook back into her book bag.

"I thought I did too. I just liked him a lot."

She closes her locker, grabs her book bag and starts to walk to her first period class.

"I'll see you two in Bible class."

"Okay," Brianna and Casey reply as they walk toward the bookstore.

Kayla is walking into algebra class when Chaz stops her. Kayla takes a step backward into a defensive stance. Chaz has never spoken to her before and she knew that he was one of Mark's best friends.

"Hey Kayla, how is my boy Mark doin?" he asked.

"I don't know; I haven't seen him."

"So it's like that," he replied looking at her coldly.

"You're not going to see about the guy you said you loved. Man, you must be bitter."

"Not bitter, better. Better now that we are not together," she says with a smile.

"Well I hope you go see him." Chaz takes his seat a few rows over from hers.

"Don't count on it," she responds as she takes her seat before the bell rings.

As her teacher begins with the lesson, Kayla's mind wonders to Mark. Everyone seems so concerned. Why isn't she? Had she forgiven him as Pastor Lee had spoken about yesterday? Does she have any feelings for him?

As the students whispered around her, Kayla couldn't wait for class to be over. When the bell finally rings, Kayla puts her notes in her binder, grabs her book bag and heads to the next class. As she is repeatedly approached about Mark, she just shrugs it off. "I don't know what happened, I wasn't there." Kayla replies over and over again.

As history class draws to a close, she prepares herself for Bible class. Dreading her walk down the hall, she knows that this is the main class full of students who know how she felt about Mark before they broke up.

As she walks up the steps toward Ms. Grace's class, she sees Ms. Grace standing at the door.

"Good morning Kayla," Ms. Grace greets her wearing another navy dress and a gold scarf.

"Good morning Ms. Grace." Kayla secretly smiles to herself wondering if there were any other colors in Ms. Grace's wardrobe.

"Please wait here a moment, I want to talk to you before class starts."

Frustrated, she asks, "Is it about Mark?"

"Yes. Let me give the class today's scripture and I'll be right back."

She goes into the room and writes down the scripture on the board.

"Please read it and be ready to discuss it when I return."

She walks out of the classroom, closing the door behind her. She leads Kayla away from the door so the students would not be distracted trying to see what was going on. Kayla leans up against one of the lockers, arms folded across her chest. She's had to answer all of her classmate's questions, now she had to answer to her teacher's too. Kayla felt herself getting angry as Ms. Grace began to speak.

"Kayla, I know you and Mark broke up but you wouldn't..." she hesitates.

"Wouldn't what Ms. Grace?" Kayla's stance softened slightly as her curiosity peaked.

"Some students are saying that you had Mark beat up." Kayla burst out laughing. "Sorry Ms. Grace, but that's funny. Why would I do that when I could do it myself," she says with a cocky attitude.

"You don't know anything about it?"

"No and I'm tired of everybody asking me. I found out about it at church yesterday, just like everyone else. I don't know what happened and I'm really trying not to get involved."

"Okay, well let's go into the room," Ms. Grace replied, relieved by Kayla's answer. "I will handle any questions or comments about Mark."

"Thanks Ms. Grace." She opens the door and Kayla walks into the classroom and sits down. Ms. Grace walks toward the front of the room while Kayla ignored the stares from her fellow classmates.

Casey and Brianna look at Kayla inquiring about what just happened. Kayla gives a small smile and winks to let them know everything is okay. Chaz and Ricardo angrily look over in her direction. They believe that she is responsible for their best friend being in the hospital.

"Class, I want us to address a situation you are probably aware of. Mark Parks was assaulted pretty badly on Saturday and is now in the hospital. He will be there for a couple of weeks recuperating. Kayla became aware of the incident on Sunday. She had no prior knowledge of the assault or those involved, so please keep questions and comments to yourself or ask me. Do you understand?"

"Yes Ms. Grace," the class responds.

"Let's start with prayer before the class discussion and I will also pray for Mark."

All students bow their heads and prayer begins.

"You know you ain't right. You should go see him," Chaz whispers to Kayla.

She concentrates on her prayer and ignores him. After prayer is finished, Ms. Grace begins to ask questions about the scripture reading. A note lands on Kayla's lap. She opens it and it reads, "If you didn't have anything to do with it, why don't you go see him?" Fed up with his accusations, Kayla stands up and faces Chaz. She glares at him and says, "You are not God so don't judge me! Since you are so worried about him, you go see him and leave me alone!"

Chaz rises slowly to respond just as Casey and Brianna rush to stand at their friend's side.

"Kayla and Chaz please step outside the class," exclaims Ms. Grace as she takes a step toward Kayla. As Chaz walks through the door, he starts to wonder if Kayla may have been telling the truth all along. He realizes that he may have made a terrible mistake. The class begins to whisper and Ms. Grace asks everyone to settle down. She gives them an assignment and walks Kayla out.

"I don't know what just happened in there but you two need to show respect for the class and one another. Didn't I say that if you had any questions or comments about Mark to direct them to me? So what just happened in there?"

"I don't know." Chaz shrugged his shoulders and looked over at Kayla.

"He's been nagging me all morning and in every class about going to the hospital to see Mark. He wrote this dumb note accusing me of setting Mark up and I can't take it anymore." She hands the note over to Ms. Grace. "I'm tryin' to do right by controlling my emotions but I'm about to punch him."

"Why did you write the note Chaz?" Ms. Grace folds the note and gives him a disapproving look.

"I felt like she owed it to him. They used to be together and now they broke up and she can't go see about him. That ain't no kind of love."

"But that's a decision for her to make, not you. And since you disobeyed my directions, you will report to detention after school. Do you understand?"

"Yes ma'am."

"Now go back in there and do your work. Do not mention another word about this."

Chaz quietly opens the door and returns to his seat.

"Kayla, I'm sorry. Kids will be kids."

Not wanting to return to class after her outburst, Kayla asks, "Can I go down to the guidance office to speak with Ms. Sanders?"

"Sure," Ms. Grace goes into the classroom and gets Kayla a hall pass and collects her things. Putting her books in her book bag, Kayla gives Ms. Grace a quick hug.

"Thanks Ms. Grace."

"You're welcome. I'll see you tomorrow."

Kayla goes down the stairs to the guidance office. She knocks on Ms. Sanders' door.

"Come in."

"Ms. Sanders, can I talk to you? I have a hall pass."

Kayla shows her the pass excusing her from class.

"Sure Kayla," Ms. Sanders motions for her to take a seat while she finishes up some paperwork in a folder.

Kayla sits down and looks out the window.

"What's on your mind Kayla?" she asks as she puts the folder away.

"I cannot understand why everyone is bothering me about Mark."

"Oh, you mean about Mark being in the hospital?"

"Yes, people are asking how he is and what happened. They can't understand why I haven't gone to see him."

Looking bewildered Kayla looks at Ms. Sanders. "Ms. Grace said students were saying I had him beat up. Come on, why would I have someone do what I can do for myself?" Kayla leans back in the seat and starts to crack her knuckles. She looks at her hands and calmly folds them in her lap.

"How do you feel about what happened to Mark?" Ms. Sanders takes note of Kayla's reaction, pleasantly surprised.

"It's bad what happened, but I'm not sure how I should feel."

"It's okay to be unsure about situations Kayla, just know it's up to you if you want to go see Mark. Don't let anyone make you feel bad if you choose not to see him."

"Thanks Ms. Sanders."

Their conversation is interrupted by a small knock on the door.

"Come in."

"Good morning Ms. Sanders," Mr. Chase says as he enters the office.

"Good morning sir," he looks over at Kayla somewhat surprised to see her.

"Good morning Miss Michaels."

"Hi Mr. Chase."

"What brings you here this morning?" Ms. Sanders asks him.

"Well, I wanted to talk to you about a student, as a matter of fact Kayla, how are you dealing with the situation concerning Mark?"

"Good, it's not my problem and I have a choice if I go see him or not."

Taken aback by her answer Mr. Chase asks, "Do you know how badly he was hurt?"

"Yes."

"He had to have his jaw wired shut, two broken ribs and a fractured wrist. Those are pretty serious injuries."

"Not to be disrespectful Mr. Chase, but his getting beat up was not my fault. I went to that group session Ms. Sanders wanted me to attend on Saturday and saw a girl around my age in a nursing home because her boyfriend hit her in the head with a bat. She is in a coma and breathes through a tube. I don't want to be like that, so I'm focusing on me and trying to make myself better. I do feel bad Mark is hurt but it is not my job to take care of him."

Ms. Sanders and Mr. Chase look at one another, amazed by Kayla's response.

"It seems that you have had some changes over the weekend Kayla," Mr. Chase remarks.

"I did. I even went to church yesterday, the first time in six months. I really enjoyed it."

"What was the message?"

"Pastor Lee spoke about forgiveness."

Looking seriously at Kayla, Mr. Chase replies, "Forgiveness, wow...would you say that you have forgiven Mark?"

"I guess. I would be lyin' if I said that our break-up

didn't bother me. He was my first boyfriend. I'm just

not so sensitive about it anymore."

"I think you would benefit from some additional

counseling to help you deal with your feelings." Mr.

Chase took a seat across from Kayla's.

"Why, because I'm not all upset about Mark getting

hurt? Are you serious?"

Ms. Sanders speaks up as she sees Kayla starting to get

agitated. "I think it would be good for you to talk to

me, or someone that you feel you can share things

with."

Looking from Ms. Sanders to Mr. Chase, Kayla

responds in an exasperated tone, "I talk to God, my

Mom, Pastor Charles and Pastor Lee."

"Okay," Ms. Sanders replied.

"Look Mr. Chase, I'll continue to attend the counseling sessions we originally agreed to. Mark isn't even here and you're punishing me for what happened to him."

"I apologize for upsetting you Kayla that was not my intent. I applaud you for doing what has been asked of you and I hope that you will continue with the positive changes you've made."

"Mr. Chase, I don't want to mess up so please just trust me when I say that I am taking steps to handling my emotions more positively."

"Okay Kayla I'll trust you. However, if there is another altercation between you and another student you will be expelled without hesitation. Do you understand?"

Smiling Kayla replies, "Yes Mr. Chase. I promise I won't be any trouble."

The bell rings and Kayla asks to be excused for lunch.

She goes to her locker and grabs her purse. Casey and

Brianna walk up as she closes her locker door.

"Hey girl."

"Hey Bri-Bri."

"You okay?"

"Yep."

"Chaz is such a jerk," Casey chimes in.

"I'm not worried about him. He just needs to stay out

of my face."

Changing the subject she asks, "What's for lunch?"

"Chicken nuggets and fries."

The girls go to the cafeteria and get their lunch. Other

classmates approach their table to ask how she's doing

but no one mentions Mark. As the day comes to a close,

Kayla and her friends meet up at their lockers and head

outside toward their bus. Kayla goes to her seat and puts her head down. As the bus nears her stop, she spots one of Mark's friends, a boy she doesn't know by name. She asks the bus driver, Ms. Moms they called her, if she could stop directly in front of her house. She tells Ms. Moms that she doesn't feel comfortable getting off and Ms. Moms grants her request. As the bus rolls to a stop a few feet from her house, she jumps off and runs toward the door. Kayla doesn't stop even after hearing someone calling her name. She grabs her keys, fumbling with the lock until finally opening the door. She slams the door and locks it, trying hard to catch her breath.

"Mom, Mom!" she calls in a panic.

Valerie comes running downstairs. "What's wrong Kayla?" she asks seeing her daughter clearly distressed.

Still breathing heavily, Kayla tries to speak. "Mom, this boy...he was trying..."

"Slow down honey and catch your breath." She rubs Kayla's back.

"There was this boy at my bus stop. He is a friend of Mark's so I had Ms. Moms drop me off closer to the house. Once I got off the bus I started to run and he was calling after me. I didn't look back. I just kept running until I got home. Please Mom, check and see if he's still out there."

Kayla moves to the living room and nervously sits down on the couch. Suddenly the door bell rings and both mother and daughter jump to their feet. Mrs. Michaels grabs her and tells her to go to the kitchen and get her stick. Looking through the peephole she flings the door open as the young man Kayla described reaches for the doorbell. Seeing the stick in Mrs. Michaels' hand, he backs away from the door.

"What do you want with my daughter?" she snaps.

"I'm sorry ma'am. I, I just wanted to ask Kayla some questions about Mark."

"What is your name young man?"

"Antonio ma'am."

"Antonio, Kayla no longer associates herself with Mark nor does she know what happened to him. Please do not come to my house or come near my daughter again. Do you understand?" she asked firmly.

"Yes ma'am," he replies backing slowly down the stairs, hoping she would not come after him with her two by four.

She closes the door, turns and looks for Kayla who is standing by the kitchen door.

"Who was it Mom and what did he want?"

"He said his name was Antonio and he wanted to ask you about Mark," Valerie replied putting her stick back in the corner.

With frustration in her voice, Kayla responded, "I'm so sick of people asking me about him. All day at school kids were coming up to me or throwing notes at me. It was so crazy. Even Mr. Chase thinks I need to talk to someone about my feelings regarding Mark, just because I wasn't showing any emotions about him being hurt. I just want this day to end."

She takes her book bag up to her room and falls on her bed. Closing her eyes wishing all the drama would end; Kayla reaches over to her CD player and pushes play. As the music starts Kayla sings along.

"God, I made some terrible mistakes, gave my body and my soul away. Now coming to be whole. I need a healing for my soul, I need healing for my soul. Give me healing."

As the song continues to play Kayla begins to reminisce about being a part of the dance ministry and how dancing before the Lord let her feel free. "God," she cries out, "help me to be better. I can't deal with all the pressure of Mark's situation. Please help me."

She suddenly feels peace as the Lord begins to remind her of whose she is and that she is important to Him. God lets her know that He has never left her and if she will continue to do what is right in His sight, He will bless her. Kayla smiles and says, "Thank you Lord." Wiping her face, she sits down and does her homework. Over the next two weeks, Kayla remembers what God spoke to her and changes begin to happen in her life.

She handles the questions about Mark patiently and continues to attend domestic violence sessions at the community center. She is presented with a certificate for completion on the last day. Her mother also attended some classes at church while Kayla had rehearsal for the youth department's dance presentation for Friends and Family Day. She was given a solo for the youth dance team and was excited.

CHAPTER NINE

The morning of Friends and Family Day finally arrives at Forever Faithful Christian Center. Visitors fill every pew in the sanctuary as committee leaders busy themselves putting things in order. Down in the youth department, the young people are either practicing their parts for their skit or putting on their dance attire. Pastor Charles is in his office printing off the programs for the youth when Kayla knocks on his door.

"Good morning Miss Kayla."

"Good morning Pastor Charles. Do you have a minute?"

"Sure, what's on your mind?" He puts down the programs and gives Kayla his undivided attention.

"I'm a little nervous about my solo."

"Why, did you forget your steps?" he asking jokingly.

"No, it's just been so long since I've danced. I don't know…I'm just nervous."

"Kayla, God has given you a talent. The enemy will try to keep you from flowing in it by placing fear and doubt in your mind. You have to remember that greater is He that is in you, than he that is in the world."

"Thanks Pastor Charles, I needed that. I feel better now." She gives him a hug and rejoins the other youth. Service begins and family and friends are acknowledged for their attendance. Announcements are made and the program for the service is read. Pastor Lee comes up and speaks to the congregation.

He prays over the service and then brings Sister Lee up to emcee the program. She introduces the men's choir and after they sing, the women and children's choirs both sing selections. Pastor Charles walks to the front of the sanctuary and introduces the youth department. First up, the youth do a skit about giving their lives to the Lord. The congregation applauds them for their efforts. Finally, Pastor Charles introduces Kayla. With some nervousness she whispers to God, "*Okay God, this is for You. Please don't leave me out here to look crazy.*" The music starts and Kayla begins to walk down the aisle. She moves to the words of the song. "*Yes, I remember when I saw your face. I felt like all my wrongs were made right, as soon as I gave into You. I took one step you took two. Yes, I called on you every single day, but then I started to lose my connection to you. Now conviction is so true, now I'm running back to you. Spirit will you fall again, make me over again. I hear your voice so clear, will you please draw me near. I'm so weak restore me back to when I first believed, please fall again on me."*

She dances with such passion and grace it causes those watching to stand to their feet and applaud her although the dance isn't complete. She continues to let the music lead her as though she is talking to God through the lyrics.

"Now this ain't like me, thought I'd never leave your side but somehow guilt and shame destroyed my faith. I thought this walk would be easy, but the devil deceived me. I will learn the hard way, there's no more living life for me. Now I see if there's no you, there's no me. So I'm calling you Jesus, please rescue me. Spirit will you fall again, make me over again. I hear your voice so clear, will you please draw me near. I'm so

weak restore me back to when I first believed. Please fall on me again."

Tears begin to fall down her cheeks and soon many in the congregation wipe their eyes as well. Overwhelmed with joy and love, Kayla stops her dance and falls to her knees and weeps, quietly whispering to God, "Thank You for loving me."

Clapping begins and Kayla rises to see her mother continuing the dance she started. Smiling, she sees that her mother moves so gracefully. The entire church is standing and as the song ends Valerie walks over to Kayla, hugs her and tells her, "I love you."

They embrace and cry. Everyone is clapping in support of the union between mother and daughter. They wipe each other's tears and bow, walking up the aisle hand in hand. Pastor Lee comes forward and thanks each ministry for their participation. The altar is open for those wanting salvation or prayer. People leave their seats and come forth. After the altar call, Sister Lee comes and gives directions on the dismissal for dinner. As people leave the sanctuary and go to the fellowship hall, some stop and congratulate Valerie and Kayla on their dance.

Kayla looks at her mom and asks, "How did you do that?"

"I would wait for you after my class and watch you. God told me to join you so I did. I hope you don't mind."

"No Mom, I loved it," Kayla replied smiling at her.

"I'm going to change my clothes. Could you bring me something home? I want to go to the hospital to visit Mark."

A little surprised Valerie replies, "Sure. Do you want

me to come and go with you?"

"No, I'll walk. It's not that far."

She goes to the bathroom and changes her clothes. On

her way out she stops to talk to Mya and D'nea.

"You did a really good job today. Your mom was good

too."

"Thanks. I was really surprised by her."

Mya giggles, "I knew all about it."

Kayla looks at her, mouth wide opened in disbelief. "I

can't believe you," she replies while punching Mya in

the arm.

"Watch it; you might need anger management if you

keep it up."

They laugh and Kayla tells them bye. As she walks

down the church steps, she adjusts her book bag and

begins her journey to Faith Clinic, which was four blocks away. Along the way, she stops briefly inside a hobby store to pick something up. Going through the lobby doors of the clinic Kayla approaches the registration desk.

"Room number for Mark Parks please," she asks politely.

"Room 415 and here's a visitor's badge," the nurse replies.

Kayla takes the badge and pins it to her shirt. Remembering another ride in an elevator, she braces herself as the elevator jerks to a stop. Stepping onto the floor, she slowly makes her way down the hall to Mark's room. The door is open and the TV is playing softly.

"Hello," she calls. "Mark, are you up?"

As she turns the corner her heart begins to beat rapidly.

She sees Mark lying in bed in a semi daze. He has lost

some weight and his face is slightly bruised. His jaws

are wired shut and the cast on his arm is full of

signatures from the hospital staff.

Mark looks up at her in surprise and tries to sit up.

"Hey," Kayla smiles slightly as she walks over to his

bed.

"Hey," he mumbles back as best he can.

"Will you be getting out of here soon?" she asks, trying

to make small talk.

"Tomorrow..."

"A lot of people have been asking about you."

"Really?" he looks at her cautiously. No one had come

to visit him but Antonio and Ricardo.

"Yeah, I caught a lot of grief for not coming to see you earlier. I wasn't ready. I was still hurt and mad at you but I've changed a lot these past few weeks. I hope we can be friends, friends and that's it."

Trying to smile he nods his head, "Okay."

The room gets quiet and awkward, neither one knowing what more to say.

"I've had a long day so I'm going to leave." Kayla gets up and gets her bag.

"Thanks for coming," Mark says.

"You're welcome," she replies as she heads toward the door. Stopping suddenly, Kayla reaches in her bag and pulls something out. As she turns around and walks back to his bed, both of her hands are behind her back.

"I almost left without giving you this."

Puzzled, Mark asks, "What is it?"

She slowly pulls her right hand from behind her back and notices Mark's reaction. His eyes are big and he nervously tries to pull himself up. She walks closer to him and says, "You know, I should be angry about how things ended between us but I'm not."

Kayla swings a mini bat that she's picked up on her way to the hospital, back and forth slowly. Unsure about what she's about to do, Mark scoots over to the other side of his bed, reaching for his button to call the nurse. "Don't be scared Mark, remember I love you."

Bringing her left hand forward she drops a Bible in his lap. Mark jumps and she starts laughing.

"Oh, you thought I was going to hurt you? No, I just want you to know what love really is. Go ahead and turn to I Corinthians 13."

As he turns the pages, Kayla puts her bat in her bag and walks away. Feeling relieved that she could show Mark how she's changed, Kayla smiles as she signs out at the registration desk. She waves as she passes Mr. and Mrs. Parks coming through the doors to visit their son.

Walking through the parking lot, she hears a voice calling her name. Kayla's mom is getting out of the passenger side door of someone's car. Receiving a hug from her mother, she freezes as she hears a male voice say, "Hello Kayla."

Looking around her mom, Kayla sees her father standing on the other side of the car.

"Daddy!" she screams as she throws herself into his arms. Holding him tightly, he smiles and kisses her on the cheek.

"Come on baby," he says to her, "let's go home."

As they walk towards the car, Kayla stops with a

confused look on her face, suddenly becoming angry.

"Why did you leave us Daddy?"

Kayla's father looks over at Valerie first before turning

to Kayla. "I was upset with things at my job, and didn't

know how to handle it. This caused a lot of tension

between your mom and I and we argued constantly. I

never wanted that for our family." Shaking his head

slowly, Mr. Michaels continued," I thought that it

would be best for all of us if I just left. I never stopped

loving you Kayla."

As he takes her hand, Kayla looks lovingly up at her

father. "If you say that you love me, does that mean

you are willing to talk to Pastor Lee with Mom?"

Smiling at her, David Michaels looks at his daughter

and says, "Yes, I'm willing to talk to Pastor Lee."

Opening the car door for Valerie, then for Kayla, David

gets in the car and smiles as he sees the joy on both

Kayla and Valerie's face. As they drive off, Kayla asks,

"Mom did you get me something to eat?"

"Yes, Kayla. I figured you'd be hungry."

Are You Being Abused?

Does something about your relationship scare you? Take the most important quiz of your life and know that we're here to help you pass.

Does your boyfriend/girlfriend:

- **Look** at you or **act** in ways that scare you?
- Act **jealous** or **possessive**?
- **Put you down** or **criticize** you?
- Try to **control** where you go, what you wear or what you do?
- Text or IM you **excessively**?
- **Blame you** for the hurtful things they say and do?
- **Threaten** to kill or hurt you or themselves if you leave them?
- Try to **stop you** from seeing or talking to friends and family?
- Try to **force you** to have sex before you're ready?
- Do they **hit, slap, push** or **kick** you?

If you answered yes to even one of these, you may be in an abusive relationship. Call the National Teen Dating Abuse Helpline if you need to talk. We're here **24 hours a day, 365 days a year.** All calls and chats are anonymous and confidential.

Contact us by phone at **1-866-331-9474 (1-866-331-8453 TTY)** or chat online at www.loveisrespect.org, from 4pm – 2am CST.

Resources

Christian Coalition Against Domestic Violence
www.ccada.org

National Teen Dating Abuse Helpline
1-866-331-9474
www.loveisrespect.org

The National Domestic Violence Hotline
1–800–799–SAFE (7233)
www.ndvh.org

Ohio Domestic Violence Network
1-800-934-9840, ext. 224
www.odvn.org

Rahab's Hideaway
614-593-5033
www.rahabshideaway.org

About the Author

Kelli Bolton is a compassionate young woman with a desire to see the Word of God set the lives of His people free.

She earned an Associate's Degree in Early Childhood Development in 1998 from Columbus State Community College and a B.A. in Cross-Disciplinary Studies from Ohio Dominican University in 2004.

Kelli is a faithful member of Agape Family Worship Center under the leadership of Pastor Yolanda Tolliver where she is actively involved in ministry as an Intercessor and Youth Leader. She enjoys fellowshipping with family, friends and the Body of Christ. She is also a member of the Columbus Christian Writer's Association. She has had two articles published in the online magazine *First Lady Magazine* and is credited as a contributing author.

Kelli and her husband Vernon are deeply committed in training their three children in the way they should go in the Lord.

www.ingramcontent.com/pod-product-compliance
Lightning Source LLC
Chambersburg PA
CBHW060808120626
46557CB00001B/131